SHERLOCK HOLMES'S
BAKER STREET BOYS

Anthony Read studied at the Central School of Speech and Drama in London, and was an actor-manager at the age of eighteen. He worked in advertising, journalism and publishing and as a television producer before becoming a full-time writer. Anthony has more than two hundred screen credits to his name, for programmes that include *Sherlock Holmes*, *The Professionals* and *Doctor Who*. He has also written non-fiction, and won the Wingate Literary Prize for *Kristallnacht*.

The Baker Street Boys books, *The Case of the Disappearing Detective*, *The Case of the Captive Clairvoyant*, *The Case of the Ranjipur Ruby* and *The Case of the Limehouse Laundry*, are based on Anthony's original television series for children, broadcast by the BBC in the 1980s, for which he won the Writers' Guild TV Award. The series was inspired by references to the "Baker Street Irregulars", a group of young crime-solvers who helped the detective Sherlock Holmes in the classic stories by Sir Arthur Conan Doyle.

Other Baker Street Boys adventures:

The Case of the Disappearing Detective
The Case of the Captive Clairvoyant
The Case of the Ranjipur Ruby
The Case of the Limehouse Laundry

THE CASE OF THE
STOLEN
SPARKLERS

ANTHONY READ

Illustrated by
DAVID FRANKLAND

WALKER
BOOKS

For Rosemary

First published 2008 by Walker Books Ltd
87 Vauxhall Walk, London SE11 5HJ

2 4 6 8 10 9 7 5 3 1

Text © 2008 Anthony Read
Illustrations © 2008 David Frankland

The right of Anthony Read and David Frankland to be identified as author
and illustrator respectively of this work has been asserted by them in
accordance with the Copyright, Designs and Patents Act 1988

This book has been typeset in Garamond Book

Printed and bound in Great Britain by Clays Ltd, St Ives plc

British Library Cataloguing in Publication Data:
a catalogue record for this book is available from the British Library

ISBN 978-1-4063-0342-1

www.walker.co.uk

CONTENTS

PROLOGUE..7

STOP THAT GIRL!.. 13

A JOB FOR QUEENIE 30

THE NEW SKIVVY.. 44

"LADY M AIN'T ALL SHE SEEMS" 57

SWEEP! SWEE–EEP! 72

NEARLY AS GOOD AS A PHOTO 90

A TELEGRAM FOR MR GERALD 103

ENTER MORIARTY 114

BLEEDING HEART YARD 127

A NICE PIECE OF PIE 137

*P*olly gazed in wonder at the jewels laid out
on Lady Mountjoy's dressing table. Dozens
of emeralds set in a long, looped necklace glit-
tered green in the gas light; pearls glowed softly
white in delicate earrings; and rubies, set in
gold rings, shone a deep, warm red. But best of
all, so beautiful that they quite took her breath
away, were the diamonds sparkling like stars
on a silver headband. Where the band rose to
a point at the front, a single stone, bigger and
brighter than all the others, flashed with cold
fire. It was so lovely that the young servant girl
was almost hypnotized by it. Dreamily, she
stretched out her hand. As her fingers almost
reached the glittering jewel, she was jerked back
into reality by a harsh shout from behind her.

"Oi! Skivvy! Keep your filthy paws off them sparklers!"

Polly jumped as though she had been stung and pulled her hand away, letting out a little squeal of surprise.

"What d'you think you're doing?" The voice belonged to Violet, Lady Mountjoy's maid, who had just come into the room. Polly blushed a deep crimson as the older girl advanced towards her.

"I- I weren't doin' no harm," Polly stuttered. "I was only lookin'."

"No you wasn't," Violet snapped. "You was going to touch 'em. Look, don't touch. That's something you better learn if you're going to get on in service."

"Yes, Violet. But it's so beautiful. What is it?"

"That, my girl, is the famous Mountjoy tiara."

"What's a tiara?"

"That is. That crown thingy. And it's worth a king's ransom."

"What's a king's ransom?"

"Don't you never stop asking questions? It's a lot of money – more'n the likes of you and me *will ever see in a lifetime. Now, hurry and get that fire made up. I want you out of here before her ladyship comes back from the bathroom. She'll be wanting to get ready for the duke's ball."*

Violet gathered up a large white towel that was warming by the fireplace and hurried out as she heard her mistress calling her. Left alone, Polly couldn't resist looking at the jewels one more time. Glancing quickly over her shoulder to make sure no one was watching, she stretched out a finger and let it rest for a moment on the big diamond in the tiara. Then, sighing deeply, she turned away, picked up her heavy brass bucket, and began placing lumps of coal on the fire in the ornate little grate.

Stepping out of Lady Mountjoy's room when she had finished, Polly almost bumped into the portly figure of Mr Harper, prowling noiselessly along the corridor. The butler let out an annoyed grunt and straightened his tailcoat.

"What are you doing up here, girl?" he demanded in his light Scottish accent.

Mr Harper was so grand that Polly found it hard not to curtsy to him. Instead, she swallowed hard and answered nervously, "Makin' up her ladyship's fire, Mr Harper. She rang for more coals."

"Very well. See to the fires in Mr Gerald's room and also the library and drawing room before you go back below stairs."

"Yes, sir."

"Just a moment."

"Yes, sir?"

"Where are your gloves? You've been told before, when you are handling coals you must wear gloves."

Polly looked down at her hands. The fingers were black with coal dust. Blushing, she tried to wipe them on her apron.

"Sorry, Mr Harper, sir. I forgot."

"'Forgot' is not good enough, my girl. You must have clean hands at all times in this household."

"Yes, sir."

"I shall speak to you about this later. Now, get on – and look sharp about it."

Polly was quite out of breath when she got back to the kitchen after making up the fires, and she was nervous about what Mr Harper would say to her. Mrs Ford, the cook, was busy dusting flour from her hands, having just put the pastry top on a large, round pie. Mrs Ford was famous for her pies – steak and kidney, veal and ham, plum and apple – they were all delicious, and she always seemed to be baking them. She looked up and scowled at Polly.

"You've took your time, young lady. What have you been up to?" she snapped.

"Nothin', Mrs Ford. Only what Mr Harper told me to do – makin' up the other fires."

"Hmmph! And just look at you. Keep those filthy hands away from my pastry. Get them washed and then start clearing up in here."

"Yes, Mrs Ford. Sorry, Mrs Ford."

Polly scurried across to the big stone sink and turned on the tap. She had just put her hands in the water when the whole house echoed to the sound of someone screaming.

"That's her ladyship!" said Mrs Ford. "Quick!"

She bustled out of the kitchen, Polly following, and they rushed up the stairs as fast as they could go. Mr Harper was just ahead of them, panting with the effort. As they all reached the top, they found Lady Mountjoy standing on the landing with her hands pressed to her head. Violet was behind her in the open doorway. Lady Mountjoy's brother, Gerald, came out of his room, half dressed, and hurried to his sister.

"What is it, Belle?" he asked. "Whatever's up?"

"My jewels!" she cried. "They've gone. Someone's stolen my jewels!" And she fell to the floor in a faint.

STOP THAT GIRL!

"Sweep! Swee–eep!" Wiggins and Gertie could hear the chimney sweep's cry echoing along the street before they saw him. He was wearing a battered top hat and dusty black tailcoat – the traditional sweep's outfit – and pushing a hand-cart loaded with brushes and poles and sacks.

"Wotcha, Charlie," Wiggins greeted him. "How's tricks?"

"'Allo, young Wiggins," the sweep replied mournfully. "Not so good – nobody round 'ere wants their chimbleys swept. Can't even find a good weddin' to go to."

"What d'you want to go to a weddin' for?" Gertie asked, puzzled.

"Don't you know nothin'?" Charlie gave her a withering glance.

"People think a sweep brings good luck to the happy couple," Wiggins explained. "Ain't that right, Charlie?"

"Right. And they slips me a nice tip for turnin' up outside the church."

"What, just for turnin' up?"

"That's right. I even gets to kiss the bride, sometimes," he grinned. "Just a peck on the cheek, mind. For luck."

Gertie pulled a face at the thought of being kissed by Charlie, who had to be at least forty years old – his skin was wrinkled and pitted with years of soot from the chimneys he swept.

"Some folk'll do anythin' for luck," she said. "My da and me used to flog bits of heather and say they was lucky. They was for us!"

"Yeah. Money for old rope," agreed Wiggins.

"What's rope got to do with it?" Gertie asked.

"It's just a saying. Money for nothing."

"Oh, right. Yeah, it was." Gertie laughed. "Money for old rope… It was just bits of heather we picked on the common."

"You a gipsy, then, lad?" asked Charlie.

"No, I'm not. My da's a tinker."

"And she ain't a lad, neither," said Wiggins. "She just likes to think she is."

"Well, I never," said Charlie. "You could have fooled me, right enough."

Gertie grinned. She was pleased to be mistaken for a boy, as she usually was, wearing ragged trousers and a jacket instead of a dress, and with her hair cut short. "I can do anythin' a boy can do – an' better," she liked to brag. And so she could. After her mother had died when she was little, her father had always treated her like a boy. Gertie had learned to climb and swim, to ride and fish and hunt for food in woods and lakes and rivers, while they travelled the country lanes in their caravan, mending pots and pans and doing odd jobs.

"And where might your father be now?" Charlie wanted to know.

"In prison."

"What for?"

"Takin' pheasants and fish off some lord's land."

"Right. Poaching, eh?"

"It ain't fair, so it ain't. Didn't they have plenty

to spare, and us with our bellies empty?"

"That's life, love. Most of the time it ain't fair. You has to make the best of it." Charlie took hold of the handles of his barrow again, ready to move on. "So long, now. Be good – and don't go poachin' no salmon outta the River Thames, eh? You might end up in the Tower of London!" Chuckling at his own joke, he continued down the street, calling "Swee–eep! Swee–eep!" again.

Wiggins and Gertie headed back towards HQ, the secret cellar where they lived with the other Baker Street Boys. But they had not gone far when the front door of a nearby house was flung open and a girl of about their own age ran out and careered down the steps, hitching up her brown servant's dress as she ran. Her white cotton cap flew from her head and her dark ginger curls tumbled down her back as she raced off along the street as though her life depended on it. A moment later, a middle-aged police sergeant and a fat constable came out of the door, waving and shouting.

"Stop that girl!" the sergeant yelled. Seeing the

two Boys, he pointed and called to them, "After her! A shilling if you catch her!"

"A bob?" Wiggins responded. He winked at Gertie and jerked a thumb in the direction the girl had taken. "Right, sir. Leave it to us!"

They set off quickly and soon disappeared round the corner, leaving the two policemen puffing behind them. When the cops rounded the corner a few moments later, they found Wiggins sitting on a pile of sacks beside Charlie's barrow, nursing his left foot, while the sweep bent over him making sympathetic noises.

"Ow, ow," Wiggins groaned loudly. "My ankle – I done my ankle in…"

"Never mind that," the sergeant said. "Which way did she go?"

"Ooh, ooooh…" moaned Wiggins, holding his foot. "What about my shilling?"

The sergeant dug into his pocket and produced a sixpence, which he held out to Wiggins.

"You haven't caught her, but you can have a tanner for trying. Come on, lad. Which way?"

"That way, sir. Look, there she goes!" Wiggins pointed down the street to where Gertie beckoned excitedly before disappearing round the next corner. The sergeant tossed the sixpence to Wiggins and set off again, followed by the puffing constable. When they were safely out of sight, Wiggins got to his feet and pulled back the sacks to reveal Polly crouched beneath them.

"It's OK," he told her. "They've gone."

"Oh, thank you, thank you both," she panted, still out of breath.

"That's all right," Wiggins grinned. "Ain't it, Charlie?"

Charlie shook his head and gave him a wry look. "You'll get me hanged one of these days," he told him. "Go on, get out of 'ere afore they comes back."

"They'll not be back in a hurry. Not with Gertie leading 'em astray." Wiggins turned back to Polly, who was starting to cry.

"Now then, there's no need for that," he said. "You're with friends now. We'll see you right."

"I don't think you can," she sobbed. "I don't think anybody can."

"Why? What you done?"

"I ain't done nothin'."

"Why was they after you, then?"

"They think I'm a thief. But I'm not. I'm innocent, honest!"

"In that case, love, you've come to the right person."

"Why? Who are you?"

"Arnold Wiggins, at your service. Captain of the Baker Street Boys, special assistant to Mr Sherlock Holmes, the greatest detective in the world. You can call me Wiggins – everybody does. Come on, let's get you to HQ and you can tell me all about what it is you ain't done."

"Is this where you live?" Polly asked as Wiggins led her down the steps.

"That's right," he replied, opening the door with a flourish. "This is headquarters – HQ for short. And here's the rest of the Baker Street Boys."

Polly stared around in surprise at the cellar and the boys and girls gathered there. Queenie, the eldest girl, was busy cooking a stew, which smelt surprisingly good. In one corner, two boys, Shiner and Sparrow, were locked together in a wrestling match that was probably friendly, though it was hard to tell since they were both putting all they had into it. Acting as referee was a bigger boy, Beaver, who wore an old-fashioned furry top hat on the back of his head. At the big old table in the middle of the room, Rosie, a pretty, golden-haired girl, was clearing faded bunches of flowers from a tray.

"Everybody!" Wiggins called out. "Listen. This is Polly. She needs our help."

The Boys all stopped what they were doing and looked at their visitor, excited at the prospect of a new case. Polly smiled nervously at them.

"You'll be safe here," Wiggins told her. "It's our secret hideaway. Nobody knows where it is, 'specially not the coppers."

"Can I stay?"

"Course you can. Right, everybody?"

The others agreed and gathered round to greet her, but Shiner hung back. "Depends who's after 'er," he grunted. "And what she's done."

"Shiner!" Queenie scolded him. "If she needs our help, she's welcome."

"It's the coppers that's after her," Wiggins

answered. "And she ain't done nothing. Which is what we're gonna prove."

"If she ain't done nothin'," said Beaver, looking thoughtful, "then why are the coppers after her?"

"Good question, Beav," said Wiggins. He turned back to Polly. "What do they say you've done?"

"They say I stole her ladyship's tiara."

"What's a tarara?" asked Rosie.

"I know a song about that," Sparrow piped up. *"Tarara-boom-de-ay, tarara-boom-de-ay..."* he sang. "I heard Miss Lottie Collins sing it on the stage once. Brought the house down, as they say."

"No, no. Not *tarara*, it's a *tiara*," Queenie corrected.

"What's that, then?"

"It's what posh ladies wear, like a sort of little crown, only just on the front half of the head."

"Sort of half a crown, then," Sparrow grinned. "Half a crown, two shillings and sixpence..."

The others groaned at his weak joke.

"Sparrow!" Wiggins admonished. "This is serious."

"Is it worth a lot of money?" Shiner wanted to know.

Polly nodded miserably. "A fortune," she said. "It's all silver and diamonds. The most beautiful thing I ever did see."

"Ah," said Wiggins. "So you have seen it?"

Polly nodded again.

"On Lady Mountjoy's dressin' table with all the rest of the jewels. While I was makin' up the fire in her bedroom."

"Cor," exclaimed Rosie. "Fancy havin' a fire in your bedroom!"

The Boys all looked impressed at the thought.

"And servants to make it up for you," added Beaver with a dreamy expression on his face.

"Never mind that," said Wiggins. "Where was her ladyship while you was looking at her spar-klers?"

"In the bathroom, with Violet. Violet's her maid."

Wiggins stroked his chin thoughtfully as he tried to picture the scene.

"I see," he said. "You was on your own in the bedroom with the jewels?"

"Yes."

"So you could've taken 'em?"

Polly burst into tears. "That's what they all say," she sobbed. "But I didn't. I'm not a thief, I'm a good girl."

Queenie put her arm round Polly, and sat her down at the table.

"Yes, of course you are, my love," she said. "Wiggins, how could you?"

"I'm not saying she did it," Wiggins replied calmly. "Only that she could've – if she'd wanted to."

"But I *didn't* want to," Polly cried. "What would I do with a diamond tiara and all them jewels?"

"You could sell 'em," Shiner said.

"That's right," added Beaver, his eyes lighting up. "If they're worth a fortune like you said, you could take 'em to a jeweller's shop and he'd give you lots and lots of money and you wouldn't never have to be nobody's servant again and you could buy a nice house and we could all come to live in it with you and have plenty to eat and bedrooms with fires in 'em and…"

"Beaver!" Wiggins said, stopping him before he got completely carried away "She ain't got them."

"No, course not. I was just thinkin'…"

"Well, don't."

"Oh. Sorry, Wiggins. Sorry, Polly."

The servant girl managed a weak smile. "'S'all right, Beaver. I know you didn't mean it."

Beaver turned bright red, but his blushes were saved by Rosie.

"Ssh!" she said, holding up her hand. "Somebody's comin'…"

Everyone held their breath and listened. They heard feet on the steps outside, and then the door opened.

"What's up with you lot?" demanded Gertie as she entered. "You look like you seen a ghost or somethin'."

"We thought you might be the coppers," said Rosie, relieved. "Lookin' for Polly."

"No chance," Gertie laughed. "They're miles away. I led 'em all over town 'fore I left 'em the other side of the park."

"Well done, Gertie," congratulated Wiggins.

"You done a great job."

"Yes," Polly said gratefully. "Thank you. Thank you both. They'd have caught me, sure as eggs is eggs, if you hadn't come to my rescue. They'd have locked me up in prison for years and years."

"Nobody's gonna lock you up in prison," Beaver told her. "Not now you got the Baker Street Boys on your side. Right, everybody?"

The others nodded their agreement.

"You're very lucky," Wiggins said. "We don't happen to have a case on just now. So we can start right away."

"Can we have somethin' to eat, first?" Gertie asked. "That stew smells good and I'm starvin' after all that runnin' about."

"Good idea," said Shiner, who was always hungry, even when he hadn't been running about. "Polly can tell us all about it while we're eatin'."

Queenie served up the stew and everyone tucked in apart from Polly, who was too upset and worried to eat. She told them how she had been in service at Mountjoy House for about six months as a skivvy, the lowest of all the servants. She had been taken on as a 'tweeny – a between-floors maid – but soon found that she had to do the work of a scullery maid and general dogs-body as well, as Lady Mountjoy couldn't afford to keep a full staff.

"So how many servants they got in that house?" Wiggins asked.

"Just the four of us since Lord Mountjoy died," Polly said. "The butler, Mr Harper; the cook, Mrs Ford; Violet, her ladyship's maid; and me."

"Sounds like a lot of people to look after one lady," said Rosie.

"There's her brother as well. Mr Gerald. And her stepson, Maurice, but he's away at boardin' school most of the time."

"Still sounds a lot to me," said Sparrow.

"It's not enough for a house that size. I have to work all the time, from the crack of dawn till last thing at night."

"Was everybody in the house when the jewels went missing?" Wiggins asked.

"Yes. 'Cept Master Maurice, of course."

"And nobody else?"

"No."

Wiggins looked serious as he considered this.

"So if you didn't take the jewels, it must have been one of them."

"I s'pose so, yes."

"Ain't no suppose about it. It had to be."

The Boys all stared at Wiggins, deeply impressed. Shiner even stopped eating, his spoon halfway to his mouth.

"Cor," Beaver said. "That's dead clever, Wiggins. You solved the case already! Mr Holmes couldn't have done no better."

Wiggins looked at him and sighed. "I only said *one* of 'em, Beav. I didn't say which one."

"Oh. Right. So which one was it?"

Wiggins closed his eyes for a moment and shook his head gently.

"I dunno," he replied. "That's what we gotta find out."

Then he had a sudden thought and turned to Polly. "If there was all them other people in the house, why did the police think *you* done it?"

"They said it had to be an inside job –

somebody what was inside the house, like you said. And they said because none of us had been out since the jewels went missin', they must still be somewhere in the house."

"That sounds right," said Wiggins. "So what did they do then?"

"They said they needed to search the house. They started at the top – that's where I sleep, in the attic, with Violet. And they looked in my box by my bed, and ... and..."

Polly broke off, sobbing so hard she couldn't speak. Queenie squeezed her shoulder comfortingly. "What did they find?" she asked gently.

"I didn't put it there. I don't know how it got there, honest...'

"What did they find?" Queenie repeated.

"They found ... they found one of her ladyship's pearl earrings. In my box, where I keep all my things."

There was a gasp from all the Boys.

"What was it doin' there?" Rosie asked.

"I dunno," Polly sobbed. "Really I don't."

Wiggins nodded solemnly. "Somebody's trying to frame you," he said.

"What, like make a picture of her?" asked Sparrow.

"No. Framing somebody means planting evidence to make 'em look guilty when they ain't."

"Right," said Beaver. "So somebody must've planted that earring in Polly's box."

"Exac'ly. It was put there on purpose so the coppers would find it ..."

"... and think Polly had pinched it?"

"Exac'ly."

The Boys were silent.

"That's awful," said Gertie. "Who'd want to do a terrible thing like that?"

"The one what really pinched the jewels," Wiggins said. "And *that's* the one we gotta find."

A JOB FOR QUEENIE

Wiggins hardly slept all night. He sat in his special armchair with his deerstalker hat pulled down over his head, sucking at his empty pipe, thinking hard. He would have taken his problem to Mr Holmes, but he knew the great detective was away, working on a case. In fact, only the day before, Wiggins had reported to him at Number 221b with some information regarding an important case Mr Holmes was working on. The information had been so significant that Mr Holmes had left to investigate it at once and would now be working under cover (or, as he put it, "incognito") for several days. So Wiggins would have to solve Polly's problem himself.

Polly didn't sleep much either. Queenie had made up a bed for her alongside her own, but although she was exhausted after all that had happened, Polly couldn't stop worrying, and wondering who was trying to put the blame on her for the robbery. Wiggins had asked her to tell him all about the other people in Mountjoy House, but the servant girl couldn't imagine which of them would do something so horrible.

Next morning, all the Baker Street Boys were up early, even before Rosie left for Covent Garden market to buy her flowers for the day.

"The answer," said Wiggins, as they gathered around the table, "has got to be in that house. I'd find it in no time if I could only get inside…"

"But you can't, can you?" Queenie asked him.

"No," he replied. "But *you* could."

"Me?" Queenie stared at Wiggins in horror. "How?"

"Easy. With Polly gone, they're gonna be needing a new skivvy to take her place, ain't they?"

"You mean you want me to…?"

"That's right. All you gotta do is roll up at the front door and—"

"No, no, not the front door," Polly interrupted. "You'd have to go to the kitchen door. Servants and tradesmen aren't allowed to use the front door."

"OK. You roll up at the kitchen door and you say you've heard as there might be a job going – and that if there is, you'd like it."

"I don't think I *would* like it. Not from what Polly's told us."

The others laughed. Then Shiner spoke up. "'Ang on a minute," he said. "If Queenie goes there, who's gonna look after us 'ere?"

"Trust you to think about that," said Sparrow. "All the same, who *is* gonna look after us? Last time Wiggins and Beaver cooked anythin' they burnt the bottom out of Queenie's best pan."

"Right," chuckled Rosie, as she headed for the door. "And they was only tryin' to boil water."

"OK, OK," said Wiggins. "That's enough of that. It'd only be for a few days and I dare say Polly can do a bit of cooking, what with having worked in a kitchen. Right, Polly?"

"Ooh, I never got to cook nothin'," Polly replied. "Mrs Ford wouldn't let me touch the food, 'cept to fetch and carry, and peel the spuds and suchlike. But I can try," she added.

"And I can do a bit," Gertie chipped in.

"If we all do a bit," said Beaver, "we'll be all right. And, like Wiggins says, it won't be for long. Once Queenie's inside that house she'll soon do what has to be done. Won't you, Queenie?"

"Course I will. Er, what *does* have to be done?"

"All you got to do," Wiggins told her, "is be my eyes and ears, like Mr Holmes always says to us. Look and listen, and then tell me what you see and hear."

"How am I goin' to tell you, if I'm stuck inside?"

"She's right," said Beaver. "I don't s'pose they'll let her nip out to come back here and report to you."

"No, they won't," Polly agreed. "She won't be allowed out at all, 'cept on errands."

"Well, if Queenie can't come to us," Wiggins said, "then we'll have to go to her."

"But we won't be able to get in," argued Shiner.

"We don't have to get in," Wiggins explained patiently. "All we have to do is wait outside in the street. Queenie'll have to come out of the kitchen door to fill a bucket from the coal cellar or put rubbish in the dustbin. Right, Polly?"

"That's right," said Polly. "I'm always goin' in and out of the kitchen. You could talk or pass a message through the railings, easy."

"There you are, then," Wiggins announced. "What we got to do is always have one of us hanging about in the street outside. If we take it in turns, they won't notice and get suspicious."

Polly was quite amazed at Wiggins's cleverness. Realizing how lucky she had been to find the Baker Street Boys, she began to feel more hopeful. Perhaps they really would be able to prove that she was innocent. Just being with them at HQ made her feel safe. It was like being back home, for she came from a large family. Indeed, it was so large that she had had to get a job as a housemaid, "going into service" as it was called, because her parents couldn't afford to feed and clothe them all. Their tiny cottage had been so crowded that Polly and her brothers and sisters had had to sleep five to a bed. Even so, she missed them terribly, only seeing them on the one day each month that she was allowed off from work. Thinking about them now brought tears to her eyes.

"Now then," Queenie reassured her. "No need to cry, my love. It'll be all right, you wait and see."

"Just leave it to us," Beaver joined in, smiling kindly at her. "We'll get it sorted. Promise."

"I was thinkin' about my family. What's my mum and dad goin' to think of me?"

"They'll know you ain't done it."

"I wish I could see them," she sniffed. "I wish I could go home."

"Well, you can't," Wiggins said firmly. "First place the coppers'll look for you. I wouldn't be surprised if they ain't been round there already."

"Oh, no," Polly cried. "The shame of it!"

"Wiggins is right," said Beaver. "You gotta lie low. Stop here and don't even poke your nose outside the door."

"Tell you what," said Queenie. "You tell us where your family lives, and one of us'll go and see 'em, all secret like, and let 'em know you're safe and that you ain't done nothin'. How's that sound?"

"I'd like that," Polly said, drying her eyes and managing a little smile.

"I'll go!" Sparrow and Gertie both volunteered together. "Me! Me!"

"Why don't you both go?" Wiggins said. "And while you're there, find out if the coppers have been, and what they said. OK? We need to know what they're up to."

Everyone was eager to leap into action. Polly told Sparrow and Gertie where to go and how to get there – it was quite a long way away – and they set off at once. Shiner looked quite grumpy, as he would have liked to go too, but Wiggins told him that he was needed – to take the first watch on Mountjoy House, setting up his shoe-shine box in the street nearby. This made him feel better at once, and more important.

"Keep your eyes peeled," Wiggins told him, "and watch everybody what goes in or out of that house. 'Specially if they look suspicious, like they might be carrying valuable jewels."

"How will I know that?" Shiner asked.

"Just keep a lookout for anything unusual," Wiggins said. After Shiner had left, he turned to

Queenie and Polly. "Now then," he said. "Let's get Queenie ready."

Queenie pushed open the black iron gate and walked down the stone steps to the kitchen door in the basement of Mountjoy House. Her heart was thumping in her chest with nerves, but she took a deep breath, straightened her dress, and reached for the brass handle of the bell pull at the side of the door. She hesitated nervously. Wiggins, trying to look casual as he leant against the railings above her, signed to her to pull it. When she did, she heard the bell tinkle inside the house.

The door was opened by a young woman wearing a maid's uniform: a long grey dress, a white apron and a frilly lace cap. She seemed a bit flustered, with strands of her dark hair escaping from her cap and clinging to her flushed face. She looked Queenie up and down and raised her eyebrows snootily. Queenie was glad she had put on her best dress. She had dug it out of the box of clothes that Mr Holmes had bought for the Boys to wear when he had taken them to eat in a hotel as a reward for helping him. But the maid, whom she guessed must be Violet, did not seem to be impressed.

"Yes?" Violet snapped. "What d'you want?"

Queenie swallowed hard and tried to remember what Wiggins had told her to say.

"Er," she hesitated, "I heard tell as you might be needin' a new maid…"

Violet stared at her suspiciously.

"Where d'you hear that?" she asked.

Queenie thought frantically. This was something she and Wiggins hadn't expected. She would have to be careful not to let on that she knew Polly.

"Er," she hesitated again, "the milkman?"

Violet snorted. "He's got a big mouth, that one. I'll have to have words with him."

"No! Don't," Queenie said quickly.

"Why not?"

"I, er, I don't want to get him into trouble."

"Hmmph! Well, as it happens we are a little short-handed."

"You mean there's a job goin'?"

"There might be a vacancy. But it's not for me

to say. You'll have to speak to Mrs Ford. This way, come on."

Queenie followed Violet into the house and found herself in the large kitchen. There was a huge black range along one wall, with a fire burning in it and lots of pots and kettles simmering on top. On another wall hung what seemed like dozens of pans, some of them black with years of use and others gleaming brightly. On a third wall plates and bowls and dishes were stacked on shelves – there were so many that Queenie thought you could feed an army off them. More plates and pots were piled up in the big sink under the window. In the middle of the room was a huge table, its wooden top scrubbed white as snow. And at this stood Mrs Ford, a plump, middle-aged woman with grey hair swept up in a bun on top of her head and a face that reminded Queenie of a bulldog that had once tried to chase her in the park. The cook was busy rolling out pastry to line a large tin, for a pie.

"Who's this?" she barked, pointing her rolling pin at Queenie. "What does she want?"

"Please, ma'am," said Queenie. "I'm lookin' for a job."

"What sort of job?"

"I don't mind. 'Tweenie. Skivvy. I'll do anything."

"What's your name?"

"Queenie, please, ma'am."

"Queenie?" Violet scoffed. "What sort of a name's that?"

"It's what everybody calls me."

"It's not a proper name. What was you christened?"

"Victoria, miss."

"Victoria. That's better."

"Yes," Mrs Ford chuckled. "You can't get more proper than that. And you don't have to call Violet 'miss', never mind her uppity ways. She's just a servant, like the rest of us."

Violet glared at her. "I'll have you remember I'm a lady's maid, not a skivvy. And I'm not going to go on doing a skivvy's jobs as well as my own. So you better find a replacement for Polly – and quick."

Mrs Ford put her hands on her broad hips and glared back at Violet.

"And I'll have *you* remember, my girl, that *I'm* the housekeeper here, and *I'm* in charge." She turned back to Queenie and looked her over carefully. "Now then, young Queenie Victoria, have you ever done this sort of work before?"

"No, ma'am. But I took care of the house when my ma was sick and looked after her and my little brother."

"And where's your mother now?"

"She died."

"I'm sorry to hear that. And that's why you need a job?"

"Yes, ma'am. And a place to live. I'll work real hard, and I'm a quick learner."

"Well, you look like a clean and decent girl. Have you got a reference?"

Queenie looked puzzled and shook her head. "No. I haven't got one of them," she confessed.

"Well, I can't give you a job without one. There's too many precious things in this house, and we've already had one thief."

"What's a reverence?" Queenie asked Polly, back in HQ. She'd already asked Wiggins and Beaver, and neither of them knew. Beaver thought it might be some sort of vicar or bishop, but that didn't make much sense.

"D'you mean a reference?" Polly replied. "It's like a letter. From somebody that knows you, saying you're all right and can be trusted."

"That's easy, then," said Beaver. "I know you and I can write you a letter like that."

"No, it has to be from somebody respectable, like a schoolteacher or a vicar. And it has to be on proper paper – in pen and ink and all that."

"Did you have one when you got your job?" Wiggins asked.

"Yes. From my old teacher."

"Well, that's no good to us," said Queenie. "I ain't got one of them. Sorry, Polly. Looks like it ain't gonna work."

There was a moment's gloom before Wiggins suddenly perked up. "Oh yes, it is," he said with a grin.

"I have known Queenie Davies for some time," Mrs Ford read aloud, holding the letter up to the light and peering through the steel-rimmed

spectacles perched on the end of her nose. *"She is honest, reliable and hard-working, and may be trusted in every respect."* She passed the letter to Mr Harper, who was standing beside her, and he read it for himself and nodded with satisfaction.

"An excellent reference," he said in his plummy voice. "He appears to think very highly of you, this Dr Watson."

"Thank you, sir," Queenie replied. "I think very highly of him, too. He's a very kind gentleman."

"Very well. If Mrs Ford approves, I think we may say the position is yours. Ten pounds a year and all found, the last Sunday in each month free. Starting immediately."

"Oh, thank heaven for that," cried Violet. "I won't have to do no more washing-up or coal heaving!"

Queenie smiled broadly and thanked Mr Harper – but as she looked at the pile of dirty pots and plates in the big sink, she began to wonder just what she had let herself in for. Saving Polly was obviously going to be very hard work.

THE NEW SKIVVY

Violet led Queenie out of the kitchen and up the steps to the grand entrance hall, and then up two more flights of stairs to the second floor. As they reached the second-floor landing, a door opened and a smartly dressed young man in his twenties came out, smoothing back his dark, wavy hair.

"Hello, Violet," he drawled, stroking his moustache with one finger. "What have we here?"

"This is Victoria, Mr Gerald. The new skivvy."

"Hmm. I hope this one hasn't got sticky fingers." He looked Queenie up and down and nodded. "I dare say she'll do. Victoria, eh? What do we call you? Vicky?"

Queenie stole a quick glance at Violet and replied, "Everybody calls me Queenie, sir."

"Ha! Yes – Queenie Victoria – very good. Queenie it shall be, then. Well, Queenie, are you a good girl?"

"I always try to be, sir."

"Ha, ha!" he laughed. "That's the spirit." With that, he winked at Violet and bounded off down the stairs.

Violet looked daggers. "Queenie!" she hissed. "It's such a common name."

Queenie shrugged. "It's what my ma always called me. What did he mean about sticky fingers?"

"Stealing things. They stick to your fingers, see. I hope you don't take things that don't belong to you?"

"No, I don't!"

"The last girl did. She was a bad lot. Helped herself to her ladyship's jewels."

"Cor! Fancy that." Queenie pretended to be surprised. "What happened to her?" she asked.

"She ran off. But don't you fret, the coppers'll catch her – and when they do, she'll be for it, I can tell you."

Violet stopped outside the next door on the

landing. "This is her ladyship's room," she told Queenie.

She knocked lightly. When there was no reply, she opened it and stepped inside, beckoning Queenie to follow.

"She must be in the drawing room," she said. "But you might as well take a peep while we're here. I look after this room, 'cos I'm her ladyship's personal maid. All you have to do is sweep the carpet and keep the fire made up. Her ladyship can't stand being cold. Very warm-blooded, she is."

Queenie thought Lady Mountjoy's bedroom was the loveliest room she had ever seen. Oriental silk curtains hung at the windows and the golden-yellow wallpaper was decorated with Japanese scenes, as was the embroidered satin quilt that lay on the bed. In front of one window was a dressing table with a big mirror on top and shiny white satin drapes hanging to the floor. On the dressing table was a box lined in white silk. Its lid was wide open, showing the box to be empty.

"Is that where the jewels were?" Queenie asked.

Violet gave her a quick glance. "What d'you want to know for?"

"Just wondered. Oh, look – somebody's made a black mark there."

She pointed to a dirty mark on the white drapes.

"Don't touch that! The police sergeant said we weren't to clean it off till the inspector from Scotland Yard had seen it. That's what Polly did, when she was pinching the jewels. Proves she did it."

"Right," said Queenie innocently. "That's what they call evidence, ain't it?"

"It is. I saw her in here myself, with coal dust all over her hands from making up the fire, just before the jewels went missing."

"Yes, but what if…?"

"Never mind 'what if'. It's not your place to keep asking questions. Come along, now. Mustn't keep her ladyship waiting."

They found Lady Mountjoy in the drawing room on the first floor, standing by one of the long windows looking out onto the street. As the two girls entered, her ladyship turned towards them, the light shining on her hair and turning it into a golden halo. She was twisting a lace handkerchief between her fingers. Queenie thought she must have been using it to dab tears from her large green eyes, for her beautiful face looked troubled. Then she raised her chin and the sad expression vanished.

"Yes, Violet?" she said calmly. "What is it?"

"This is the new girl, milady. Her name's Vict—"

"Queenie," Queenie interrupted quickly. "My name's Queenie, ma'am, er, my lady."

"I once had a dresser called Queenie, and very good she was too. Well, Queenie, I hope you'll be happy with us. We have a small staff at the moment, but there's only myself and my brother to look after. And my stepson, when he's home for school holidays. So you shouldn't find the work too hard."

"No, my lady. I'm sure I won't."

"Mrs Ford will tell you your duties, of course. And Violet will show you the ropes. Right, Violet?"

"Yes, milady."

"The first thing you must do is take Queenie to

the draper's and get her fitted out with a uniform. That's a very pretty frock she's wearing, and we don't want it spoilt by housework, do we?"

Violet shuffled her feet and looked embarrassed.

"I'm sorry, milady," she said. "I don't think I can do that."

"Why ever not?"

"The draper says he won't give us any more credit."

"I see." Lady Mountjoy bit her lip and looked for a moment as though she might cry. Then she raised her chin again defiantly. "I must have overlooked the account. Very well. I shall see to it presently."

"The last girl left a dress behind, milady. I should think they're much the same size…"

"Excellent. So, Queenie. You can wear that for the time being – just until we get things sorted out, you understand."

Violet took Polly through the house and up four flights of stairs, each one narrower and plainer than the last, until they reached the attic at the very top. By then, the thick carpets on the lower floors had given way to lino and thin rugs. Five doors led off the top landing. Violet told Queenie that Mr Harper and Mrs Ford each had one of the bedrooms, and two were boxrooms used for storing things.

"And this one," she said, opening the final door, "is ours."

It was a bare room, with shiny brown lino on the floor. The striped wallpaper and the curtains hanging at the single window were faded with age. The furniture consisted of a wardrobe, a washstand with a large water jug and bowl on its marble top, two wooden chairs and two iron beds.

"That's your bed," Violet told Queenie. "And this one's mine. I hope you don't snore."

"Not that I know of," Queenie answered.

"That's good. 'Cos I like my sleep – 'specially in the mornings. You'll be getting up first, to clear out the grates and make up the fires. I get an extra half hour. So just make sure you don't wake me up, or you'll feel the rough edge of my tongue."

"Yes, Violet."

Violet opened the wardrobe. "Now then," she said, "let's see what we got here. My things are on this side. And those are Polly's."

Two dresses, a long skirt and an outdoor coat hung on the left-hand side. On the other side was a stripy skirt, a threadbare woollen coat and a brown cotton servant's dress, which Violet lifted out and held up against Queenie.

"I reckon that'll fit you, more or less," she said. "And if it don't, that's just too bad."

"Violet," Queenie asked as she started to get undressed, "what did you mean when you said the draper's won't give her ladyship any more credit?"

"It means, they won't let her have anything more on tick without paying cash for what she buys."

"Why not?"

"'Cos she owes 'em too much money already. Now stop asking questions. Get this on and look sharp about it."

Queenie quickly changed into Polly's brown dress. It was a bit big for her, but when she tied an apron round her middle it didn't look too bad.

"Well," Violet said. "You'll have to wait for your fairy godmother if you want to go to the ball. But it'll do for now, I suppose. Hang your own frock in the wardrobe, and you can put your personal things in there."

She pointed to a tin box at the foot of Queenie's bed. "There might be some of the last girl's stuff in it, but I don't suppose she'll be coming back, so you might as well have it."

Queenie stared at Polly's box. She almost asked if that was where the pearl earring had been found, but stopped herself just in time. That would have given the game away!

"Does it have a lock?" she asked.

"What you want a lock for?" Violet replied sharply. "Who d'you think's going to steal your things? Me?"

"No," Queenie stammered. "Course not."

"Cheeky madam! And anyway, what've you got that's worth stealing?"

"Nothing. I ain't got nothing."

"Right. Put this cap on, then, and we can get back to the kitchen. Mrs Ford'll be wondering where we've got to."

She handed Queenie a white cotton mob-cap and helped her tuck her hair inside it, then she led her downstairs again.

As the girls approached the kitchen, Queenie heard a voice that sounded somehow familiar. A man was standing with his back to the door, talking to Mr Harper and Mrs Ford. He turned round as Queenie and Violet entered the room, and with a shock she realized who it was.

"Ah, Violet," said Mr Harper. "This is Inspector Lestrade of the detective branch of Scotland Yard. He has come to solve our mystery. Inspector, this is Violet, Lady Mountjoy's personal maid."

Lestrade nodded to Violet and craned his neck to get a better view of Queenie, who was trying to hide behind her.

"Violet," he said. "I'm pleased to see you. I understand from Sergeant Brown's report that you were the last person to see the jewels before they were purloined."

"Yes," Violet replied. "Apart from the thief, that is. Apart from Polly."

"Quite so. And who is this young lady?

Come forward if you please, miss."

Violet stepped aside and pushed Queenie forward. Queenie pulled the mob-cap down as far as it would go and bobbed a little curtsy with her head lowered. She held her breath, fearful that the inspector would recognize her.

"This is Victoria," Violet said. "She's new – only started today."

"She comes with excellent references," said Mr Harper. "No need to be shy, girl. Hold your head up, now."

Queenie reluctantly raised her head and managed a little smile. Lestrade looked at her and frowned slightly, trying to remember where he had seen her before.

"Victoria, eh?" he said, thinking hard, then giving up. "Hmm. Well, since you were not here when the robbery took place, Victoria, I shall not need to question you. You may get on with your work."

"Starting with that washing-up," said Mrs Ford, pointing to the pots and dishes piled up in the sink.

"Yes, Mrs Ford," Queenie answered. She

hurried across the room and got to work, pleased that she would be able to listen to what the inspector said.

"I believe that the only persons in the house at the time of the robbery were the servants and the family. Is that correct?" he asked.

"That is so," Mr Harper told him. "Lady Mountjoy and Mr Gerald, the three of us, and Polly."

"And no one else could have got in?"

"Not without my knowledge, sir. There are only two doors into the house. Without a key, the front door can only be opened from the inside; and this one leads into the kitchen, where Mrs Ford was busy baking."

"So she would have seen anyone trying to come in?"

"Without a doubt."

Lestrade thought this over for a moment, pacing the kitchen.

"And the same applies to anyone trying to get out through here?" he asked.

"That's right," said Mrs Ford. "I'd have seen 'em for sure."

"Which door did Polly use to escape from the house?"

"The front door," said Violet. "I seen her run down the stairs and across the hall, with the sergeant and constable after her."

"Very good," said the inspector. "And was she carrying anything, could you see?"

"Oh, no, sir. She was empty-handed, I'm sure. And running for dear life."

"Very well. In that case, despite Sergeant Brown's thorough search, the jewels must still be somewhere in this house. All we have to do is find them, and the case is solved."

"Lady M Ain't All She Seems"

For the rest of the day, Queenie was kept very busy by Mrs Ford, washing-up and cleaning in the kitchen and running up and down stairs fetching and carrying until she thought her legs would drop off. She took regular trays of tea to Inspector Lestrade and two detectives, who were searching the house again from top to bottom, so she was able to take note of what they were doing. They did not find anything.

Queenie was in the drawing room making up the fire and cleaning the hearth when the inspector searched it, watched by Lady Mountjoy and her brother, who both looked upset and nervous. Gerald stood by his sister, holding her hand to comfort her as Lestrade pulled books from shelves, opened drawers, peered behind pictures and curtains, tapped on walls to check for secret panels, tinkled a few notes on the grand piano to make sure nothing was resting on the strings, then lifted the lid and looked inside to make doubly sure. Finally, he stood in front of the life-sized oil painting of Lady Mountjoy, dressed in a beautiful ball gown and wearing all her jewels, including the tiara, that hung on one of the walls. He examined it and shook his head.

"I believe we can be certain, my lady, that the jewellery is not in this room," he said. "It would be quite easy to hide a diamond ring, say, or even a small necklace – but not the tiara."

"What could the girl have done with it?" Gerald asked.

"That, sir, is the question. And we must also ask if the theft was planned in advance."

Lady Mountjoy looked doubtful. "I don't believe Polly was bright enough for that," she said.

"Then someone must have put her up to it," said Gerald. "Told her what to do and how to do it."

"That, sir, is a possibility. But some of these youngsters are sharper than they look, as I have discovered to my cost on several occasions."

Queenie just managed to stop herself laughing – as she knew Wiggins and the others would do when she told them what the inspector had said. But she kept quiet and hoped that none of the grown-ups would notice she was still there, and listening, as she carried out her tasks.

"Am I correct in assuming that the jewels were normally locked in the safe in the library?" Lestrade asked.

"Yes," Lady Mountjoy replied. "They were."

"And you alone had the key?"

"That is correct. I only brought them out when I was going to wear them for special occasions."

"I see. So anyone wanting to steal them without breaking into the safe would have to do it on such an occasion?"

"Yes."

"And plan it in advance."

"Or they could just see them and grab them on an impulse," Gerald said.

"And then look for a secret hiding place?" Lestrade asked. "I hardly think your maid had time for that, do you?"

At that moment, Lady Mountjoy caught sight of Queenie.

"Leave that, Queenie," she told her, "and get back to the kitchen."

"Yes, my lady."

The inspector looked round.

"Queenie?" he said. "I thought your name was Victoria?"

"Yes, sir. It is. People call me Queenie, for short, like."

"Yes, yes," said Lady Mountjoy impatiently. "Run along, now."

Queenie picked up the coal bucket and scampered out of the room. Lestrade's brow creased in thought as he watched her go, then he shrugged and turned back to her ladyship.

It was getting dark by the time Wiggins returned to HQ. When he pushed open the door, he was greeted not by the appetizing aroma of one of Queenie's stews, but the sour smell of boiled cabbage and turnips.

"Pooh!" he exclaimed, wrinkling his nose. "What a pong."

"Sorry, Wiggins," Beaver apologized. "It's all we could find."

"Yeah, I know," said Wiggins. "Ain't nobody can get stuff out of the shopkeepers like our Queenie. Never mind. Better than nothing, eh?"

He looked around the room. It was remarkably neat and tidy.

"What's been going on here, then?" he asked.

"Polly's been cleanin' up," said Beaver. "I tried to stop her, but she wouldn't listen."

"I had to do something to pass the time," Polly explained. "Hope you don't mind."

"Mind? No, course not."

"And it did need it."

"We been meaning to have a clean-up for ages, ain't we, Beav?"

"Have we?" Beaver asked, then yelped as Wiggins kicked his ankle. "Oh, yes. Yes, we have. For ages."

"But we sort of never got round to it," Wiggins went on. "Too busy solving crimes."

"I might not be much of a cook," Polly went on, "but I'm very good at housework. It's what I'm used to."

Wiggins found it hard to understand how anybody could actually *like* cleaning and tidying. But before he could say so, the door opened and Sparrow came in with a loaf of bread tucked under his arm.

"I managed to get this from the baker's," he said, plonking it down on the table. "He said it's only yesterday's, so it ain't too stale."

"Good lad," said Wiggins. "We're gonna need it."

Sparrow sniffed the air and pulled a face. "What's that smell?"

"Cabbage and turnip," Beaver told him. "And a bit of marrowbone."

"It's very good for you," said Polly. "Honest."

Sparrow was not convinced. "I might be able to get somethin' to eat at the theatre," he said hopefully.

"The theatre?" Polly asked, surprised. "What theatre's that?"

"The Imperial," he replied proudly. "I'm the call boy."

"Gosh. Do you get to meet the actors and actresses?"

"Course I do. It's my job to look after the

artistes and see they gets on stage at the right time and everythin'."

"Well, fancy that," Polly said, impressed. And then, after a pause, she added, "Her ladyship used to be on the stage."

Wiggins looked interested. "What, Lady Mountjoy? An actress?"

"That's right. Only she wasn't Lady Mountjoy then. She was Miss Belle Fontaine."

"That's posh," Beaver commented. "Sounds French."

"It'll be her stage name," said Wiggins.

"That's right," said Sparrow. "You gotta have a fancy name if you're gonna be a star."

"Her real name was probably Betsy Smith or something plain like that," Wiggins went on.

"Mr Gerald's other name is Huggett," said Polly, "and he's her brother."

"Well," Beaver joined in, "if he's her brother, and his name's Huggett, then Lady M's real name, afore she was Lady M or Belle Fontaine, must've been Huggett too. That don't sound so posh, does it?"

"Well, there you are, then," said Wiggins.

"Lady M ain't all she seems."

"No. She ain't a proper lady," Sparrow said.

"Oh yes, she is," Polly said, defending her former employer. "She's a lady through and through. The finest lady you ever could hope to meet."

When he arrived at the theatre that evening, Sparrow asked Bert, the stage doorkeeper, if he knew anything about Belle Fontaine. Bert's face took on a faraway look.

"Belle Fontaine," he sighed. "Oh, yes, I remember her. What a beauty! The stage-door Johnnies used to line up outside after the show, hopin' she'd just give 'em a smile."

"What's a stage-door Johnny?" Sparrow asked.

"Why, a young toff what hangs about the theatre trying to click with the girls."

"Is that what happened to Miss Fontaine? Did a stage-door Johnny click with her?"

"They all tried! But she could take her pick – and she did. Hooked herself a lord, didn't she."

"Was that Lord Mountjoy?"

"How d'you know that, you young rascal?"

"Oh, I, er, know a girl what used to work for her."

"What, in service, like?"

"That's right. She was a maid."

"She'll have been all right, then. Belle always treated people well – her dressers and such. Never forgot where she come from."

"Wasn't she posh, then?"

"Posh?" Bert chuckled. "Not when I first knew her, she weren't. She never had two ha'pennies to rub together. Her dad was a cabbie and her ma took in washing. But she soon learned how to put it on like a lady."

"Was she good at acting, then?"

"Good? She was a bloomin' marvel. Whatever part she was playin', you always believed every word. It was a sad day for the stage when she married a lord and gave it up."

Sparrow felt like a real detective. He was pleased with himself for finding all this out, and he would have gone on quizzing Bert but then he heard a voice calling his name.

"Sparrow? Where is that young rapscallion? Sparrow!"

It was Mr Trump, the manager of the theatre, who appeared at the end of the corridor, resplendent in his bulging evening suit, red-faced with indignation. He spotted Sparrow and bellowed furiously at him.

"What are you dilly-dallying there for, boy? Have you not taken cognizance of the fact that there are artistes awaiting your ministrations? They require comestibles and beverages, *toute de suite*!"

"The acts need food and drink, sharpish," Bert translated dryly. "Better get a move on, eh?"

Queenie was quite worn out by the time Inspector Lestrade and his policemen finally gave up their search of the house and left. She hadn't stopped working all day, and by the time Mrs Ford called her into the kitchen for supper, she was almost too tired to eat. The cook told Queenie to sit down at the big table with Violet and Mr Harper, and put a big plate of food in front of her. The food was delicious – it was one of Mrs Ford's steak and kidney pies, with lots of meat and a rich pastry crust – and Queenie was glad to eat something she had not had to cook herself. But her eyelids kept drooping and she had to blink very hard to stay awake.

"Soon as you've washed these things up, you'd better get yourself off to bed," Mrs Ford told her. "You have to be up at six in the morning. First thing, you've got to rake out the ashes from this range, clean it up and polish it with black lead. The brushes and dusters and stuff are all in that box under the sink. Then get the fire lit and a kettle of water on the hob so it'll be boiling by the time I come down. I can't start the day without my cup of tea, and neither can Mr Harper, so don't you forget that."

"No, Mrs Ford," Queenie answered. "What time does Lady Mountjoy get up?"

"Never you mind about her ladyship," Violet said sharply. "I look after her. You just try to keep out of her way."

"Her ladyship doesn't rise until about ten o'clock," Mr Harper said. "So that gives you plenty of time to dust and polish the drawing room and morning room and prepare the fires and be out of the way before she comes down. Do you understand?"

Queenie didn't really understand why she had to do everything before Lady Mountjoy got up, but she nodded and said, "Yes, Mr Harper."

"Right, then, off you go and get some shut-eye."

Queenie climbed wearily up the stairs to the attic. She was glad she did not have to carry a candle – there were gas lamps on the walls of every landing. They were turned down low, leaving large patches of dark shadow which made her nervous that someone might be lurking in them, but she could still see where she was going. The door to the drawing room was slightly ajar and, as she passed it, she could hear voices from inside. They belonged to Lady Mountjoy and Gerald, and they seemed to be raised as if in argument. Queenie stopped to listen, shrinking into the shadows and out of sight.

"It won't do, Gerald," she heard Lady Mountjoy say crossly. "It has simply got to stop."

"I have to keep up appearances, sis," Gerald replied in a whining tone. "How would it look if Lady Mountjoy's brother couldn't pay his debts?"

"You *can't* pay your debts!" she snapped back. "You expect me to pay them for you. And I don't have the money."

"You could sell something."

"You know very well I can't do that. When Henry died he left everything in this house to Maurice, to be held in trust until he comes of age."

"Maurice! I'm sick of hearing about Maurice. Your stepson can go to the most expensive school in England and have everything he wants, but your own brother has to suffer!"

"Suffer? You live here for free and get fed and clothed by me without having to lift a finger – you don't exactly suffer, Gerald."

"I will if I don't pay what I owe."

"What do you mean by that?"

"You'll see – if Bernie Blackstone doesn't get his money. You've got to help me, sis, or I'm done for. Please. I'm begging you."

There was silence for a few seconds. Then Lady Mountjoy spoke again, sounding even more vexed. "Oh, get up, Gerald. You look ridiculous on your knees like that. Get up and go to bed."

Queenie slipped away from the door before Gerald could come out and catch her, and climbed the stairs to the top landing as quietly as she could. She was so excited and puzzled by what she had overheard that her tiredness was quite forgotten.

In the bedroom, she undressed quickly and slipped into her bed, pulling the blankets up under her chin. It was far more comfortable than her makeshift bed in HQ, and she knew that she would sleep well once she got to sleep. But for the moment her brain was racing as she thought over all that had happened during an eventful day. She would have plenty to tell Wiggins when she saw him, though she struggled to make sense of what she had seen and heard. Wiggins would be able work out what it all meant, she was sure.

All was quiet and peaceful as the house settled down for the night, but Queenie was missing the other Boys and couldn't sleep. As she lay wondering what they were all doing, and how they were getting on without her, she heard someone talking quietly on the stairs. There was a giggle that sounded like Violet's, followed by a deeper, man's chuckle. Curious, Queenie slipped out of bed and crept across the room. Easing the door open, she tiptoed to the top of the stairs and peered down to the next landing. Below, she could see Gerald standing with his arm round Violet's waist, whispering something in her ear. Violet shook her head and pushed him away – though not very hard – as he tried to kiss her. Then she gathered up her long skirt and turned to climb the stairs, giggling again.

Queenie just managed to duck out of sight and scurry back to bed before Violet came in. She pulled up the bedclothes and lay quietly while the older girl undressed, humming happily to herself. Queenie recognized the tune of the popular song, "Daisy, Daisy, give me your answer, do". As she closed her eyes, more of the words ran through her mind: "It won't be a stylish marriage, we can't afford a carriage..." And then she was asleep.

SWEEP! SWEE–EEP!

Queenie slept solidly until the alarm clock woke her at six the next morning. Sleepily, she turned it off and tried to remember where she was and what she was doing there. Seeing Violet still asleep in the other bed brought everything back to her in a rush.

"Ooh," she groaned under her breath, "the blinkin' fires!"

Fighting to keep her eyes open, she poured cold water from the big china jug on the washstand into the bowl and splashed it on her face. Then she struggled into the brown dress, stuffed her hair under her mob-cap and staggered downstairs to start her duties for the day.

The kitchen was cold and dark in the dim early morning light as Queenie busied herself with cleaning out the ashes from the range and raking them through the bars into a bucket. The fine grey dust caught in her throat and made her cough, and she crossed the room to get a drink of water from the big brass tap. As she filled a mug at the sink, she looked out through the window. Someone was leaning on the black iron railings above, looking down into the kitchen. It was Wiggins.

"What you doin' here at this time of day?" Queenie asked him when she had unlocked the kitchen door and gone outside.

"That's a nice welcome and no mistake," he grinned as he climbed down the stone steps from the street. "Polly said this was the only time I could be sure of finding you on your own to talk to."

"Did she, now? You can tell her she can swap places again any time she likes."

"You ain't having a good time, then?"

"I got a nice bed to sleep in. And the grub's good – we had steak and kidney last night, and there'll be bacon and egg and sausages for breakfast this mornin'. But I don't like bein' nobody's servant, and I do miss the Boys."

"We all miss you."

"Miss my cookin', more like. What did you have for supper last night? Anythin' good?"

"Wasn't too bad, considering. Turnips and cabbage."

Queenie sniffed. "Bet my little brother didn't like that. How's he behavin' his self without me to keep him in order?"

"All right," Wiggins grinned. "For Shiner."

"Hmm. How long you reckon this is gonna take? Only I don't think I can stand too much of it."

"Depends. Have you found anything out yet?"

"Yeah, I got a lot to tell you. But I'll have to be quick."

"Go on, then. I'm all ears, as they say."

Queenie took a deep breath and told Wiggins everything that she had seen and heard the day before. He listened with great interest, and let out a low whistle when she finished.

"Blimey," he said. "Sounds like they've all got something to hide!"

"Yeah," she replied. "'Cepting her ladyship."

Wiggins shook his head. "Don't be too sure

about that. She ain't all what she seems, nei-ther."

"No!" Queenie was quite shocked. "How d'you make that out?"

"Sparrow's been asking about her in the theatre. Turns out she ain't really posh at all – her old man was a cabbie."

"I can't believe it. She's a real lady through and through…"

"It's all an act. Honest. Going by what Sparrow found out, she used to be a wonderful actress when she was on the stage. Sounds like she still is. So keep your eyes open and watch out for her."

"Right, I will."

"That's a good girl. Hello, what's this?"

He stared at the wall behind Queenie. Just above her head was a white handprint. He reached out and touched it, then examined his fingers.

"What is it?" Queenie asked. "Looks like flour."

Wiggins considered it for a moment, then shrugged.

"Yeah, it is," he said. "Never mind that. Listen.

I need to get inside the house to take a look-see for myself. There could be clues that Lestrade and his coppers have missed."

Queenie looked doubtful. "They was very thorough," she said.

"I don't care about that. I gotta see for myself, like Mr Holmes would."

"How will you manage that, then?"

"You're gonna help me."

"I can't do that!"

"Oh, yes, you can. I've worked it all out. This is what I need you to do…"

Shiner and Rosie took up their posts watching Mountjoy House again during the morning. Shiner grumbled that he was losing money because the street was so quiet that he hardly had any customers, but Beaver assured him they were doing important work. He reminded Shiner how he had helped to solve the mystery of the Ranjipur Ruby by spotting that the villain's boots were old and needed mending. Pleased that Beaver remembered his part in that case, Shiner reluctantly agreed to stay put.

Rosie was losing money too, but she was determined to do everything she could to help Polly. And in any case, she wanted Queenie back at HQ as soon as possible. She'd missed being seen off to Covent Garden in the early morning – and even one day of Polly's cooking was one too many. So as soon as she had come back from the market and tied up her posies and buttonholes, Rosie had hurried out to the street. Beaver and Gertie were already there with Shiner, and Beaver quietly told her that Wiggins had a plan. They were all to be ready for it. In the meantime, Rosie was to go on patrolling with her tray of flowers, and keep her eyes open for anything suspicious.

Nothing happened for an hour or more, and then the front door of the house opened and a youngish man came out, looked around and set off along the street. He was smartly dressed in a dark coat with a velvet collar, his hat tilted at a rakish angle, and he was swinging an ebony cane with a silver knob.

"That must be Mr Gerald," Beaver whispered to Gertie. "I'll follow him and see where he's goin'. You back me up so you can take over if he spots me."

Gerald walked past Shiner with barely a glance, which disappointed the young shoeshine boy, who prided himself on being able to judge a man's character by his boots and had hoped for a chance to get a proper look at this man's. But the dandy stopped to look at the flowers on Rosie's tray, and flashed his teeth at her in a smile.

"What are you doing here, my dear?" he greeted her. "We don't usually get flower girls in this quiet street."

Rosie thought fast. "No, sir," she replied. "That's why I thought I'd give it a go."

"Hm. Clever as well as pretty." He treated her to another, rather oily smile, picked up a red carnation and sniffed it. "I'll take this one."

He handed over two pennies, slipped the flower into the buttonhole on his lapel, and continued on his way. Keeping their distance from him and each other, Beaver and Gertie trailed after him as he sauntered along the street and round the corner. The three of them were hardly out of sight when Sparrow strolled round the corner at the other end of the street, wearing a very ragged jacket, and leant casually against the wall. When Queenie appeared briefly at a window on the second floor of the house, he gave her a surreptitious thumbs-up. She saw him, returned the signal and disappeared again. All was quiet for several minutes, then there were shouts from inside the house. Queenie reappeared at the window and flung it open. Clouds of thick brown smoke billowed out.

Sparrow slipped back round the corner. A few seconds later a familiar cry rang out: "Sweep! Swee–eep!" and a barrow came into sight, piled up with brushes and sacks. It was pushed by a young chimney sweep, his too-big tailcoat hanging loosely from his shoulders, his face blackened with soot but still recognizable, to anyone who knew him, as Arnold Wiggins, leader of the Baker Street Boys. His even younger assistant, trotting alongside the barrow and clearly enjoying playing a part, was Sparrow.

"Swee–eep! Sweep!" Wiggins cried again, very loudly, as he approached Mountjoy House.

As he did so, the basement door opened and Violet came hurrying up the steps and called him over. Parking the barrow outside and leaving it in Sparrow's care, he followed her down into the kitchen.

"Are you a sweep?" Mrs Ford asked, staring at him across the big table, where she stood next to Mr Harper.

"Yes, missus," he said cheerfully. "At your service."

"Where's the regular sweep?"

"Charlie's took sick today, missus. So I'm looking after his round for him."

"You seem very young," said Mr Harper.

"I'm not as young as I look, guv'nor. We sweeps is all short, you know. On account of when we used to have to climb up inside the chimbleys."

"Huh! A likely tale."

Mrs Ford chuckled and looked kindly at Wiggins. "You're a cheeky monkey and no mistake."

"I do my best, missus. Don't cost nothin' to be cheerful, do it?"

"Quite right," she said. Her eyes twinkled

and she gave him a motherly smile.

Mr Harper cleared his throat noisily. "You're quite sure you know what you're doing?" he asked.

"Oh, yes, guv. Served my time with Charlie, I did. Learned the trade from him."

"Excuse me, Mr Harper, but please can we get on?" Violet butted in, hopping from one foot to the other and looking agitated. "That chimney's smoking something awful. Her ladyship's room will be covered in smuts and I'll have to clean it all up."

"Sounds like you got a blockage," Wiggins said.

"But we only had the chimneys swept a month ago," Mr Harper snapped.

"Ah, in that case," declared Wiggins, tying to sound as though he knew what he was talking about, "it probably ain't a question of soot. It's most likely birds."

"Please," Violet repeated. "Whatever it is, can we hurry up and do something about it?"

"Yes, yes," Mr Harper said tetchily. "Show him where it is."

Violet led Wiggins out of the kitchen and up through the house to Lady Mountjoy's room, where they found Queenie standing guard over the fireplace. Smoke continued to pour into the room instead of going up the chimney.

"Right, what we got here, then?" Wiggins said, peering through the dense smoke and winking at Queenie. "It's like a proper London pea-souper in here, ain't it. 'Cept the fog's usually outside the house."

"Never mind making jokes," Violet snapped. "Do something about it. Quick!"

Wiggins ambled over to the fireplace, bent down and peered up the chimney.

"Can't see no daylight," he announced. "Yes, that's a blockage right enough."

"Can you fix it?"

"I'll need a number two brush for that."

"Well, have you got one?"

"Course I have. On the barrow. Why don't you nip down and tell the lad to bring it up here?"

"I'm not running up and down stairs for you," Violet snorted. "Victoria can go."

"Who?"

"That's me," Queenie said, glaring furiously at Violet.

"Victoria, eh?" Wiggins tried to keep a straight face. "That's a posh name."

"Yes, isn't it." Queenie flounced out of the room and hurried down the stairs.

Left with Violet, Wiggins looked around the room, taking everything in.

"This is nice," he said. "Who sleeps in here, then? Is it yours?"

"This is Lady Mountjoy's room."

"Lady Mountjoy? Where have I heard…? Oh, yes. Ain't this where you had that robbery?"

"How do you know that?" she demanded.

"News travels fast among tradesmen," he said, tapping the side of his nose. "But am I right?"

"Yes. From this very room, as it happens."

"Well, I never." Wiggins put on a look of surprise. "Was there much took?"

"I'd rather not talk about it, if you don't mind."

"Go on. You can tell me. I dare say it'll be in all the papers, anyhow."

Violet pursed her lips, then the temptation

to share the exciting events of the past few days became too much for her. She spoke quietly. "All her ladyship's precious jewels. Including the famous Mountjoy tiara, what can't be replaced."

"And they was all in this room?"

"In that satin jewel box over there on the dressing table."

Wiggins strolled over to look more closely.

"Don't touch anything!" Violet warned him. "I don't want anything else to clean. The girl that took them left a dirty mark on the drapes."

"Yes, so I see," said Wiggins, bending to examine the black fingermarks on the dressing table. He grinned and held up his own sooty fingers. "When you're a sweep, you soon learn to keep your hands to yourself."

He moved to the open window, leant out and looked down. Below him he saw Queenie come out of the kitchen and climb the steps from the basement to the street, where Sparrow was lounging against the barrow. He watched as they spoke, then he called down to Sparrow.

"A number two brush, lad! Yes, that's the one – that's all we'll need. And a sack. Bring 'em up here, now! Quick as you can!"

Sparrow pulled a sweep's brush from the bundle, took a sack from the barrow and headed back down the steps into the kitchen behind Queenie. Wiggins turned back to Violet.

"You say it was a girl what took the jewels?" he asked.

"That's right. The skivvy."

"Cor. Not her?" He jerked his thumb towards the window and Queenie. "What d'you call her, Victoria?"

"Don't be daft. The girl what was here before her."

"Oh, I get you. Did you see her take 'em?"

"Course I didn't. I'd have stopped her, wouldn't I?"

"Yeah. Course you would. Er, how d'you know it was her, then?"

"It had to be. I was only out of the room for a couple of minutes."

"Why? Where was you?"

"With her ladyship in the bathroom, just down the corridor there."

"You don't think somebody else might've got

in and nicked 'em, while you was gone?"

"No chance. Hey, you're worse than the inspector, you are. Questions, questions…"

Wiggins stopped short. Had he given himself away? He grinned at her. "You sound just like my ma – she used to say I wanted to know everything. 'Arnie,' she used to say when I was little, 'I don't know what we're gonna do with you, always askin' questions.'"

"You haven't changed much, then, have you? You ought to be a detective, like that Mr Whatsisname – Hemlock Bones, is it?"

"Sherlock Holmes?"

"That's the one. We could do with him round here now. To tell us what that wicked Polly's done with her ladyship's jewels."

"You don't need him," Wiggins joked. "Give me a bit of time and I'd soon find 'em for you. P'raps she stuffed 'em up this chimbley…"

"You ain't going to find 'em up there," Violet laughed. "That was the very first place the inspector looked."

Just then, Queenie returned with Sparrow, carrying the brush and sack.

"Violet," Queenie said, "her ladyship's calling for you. She's in the drawing room."

"Right," Violet answered. "You stay here and keep an eye on this one. He's too sharp for his own good. And make sure neither of them touches anything."

As Violet hurried away down the stairs, Sparrow looked around the room with his mouth wide open.

"Cor," he breathed. "Fancy havin' a bedroom like this."

"Nice, ain't it?" Queenie said. "And all to yourself."

"Yeah. I bet that bed's real soft and comfy."

Queenie just managed to stop him as he walked towards the big bed to test it.

"Don't touch!" she warned. "Or I'll be in real trouble."

"Yeah," Wiggins added. "We ain't got time for that. Let's get this chimbley cleared."

"Try not to make a mess," Queenie told him. "I'm the one what'll have to clean it up."

"I'll do my best, miss," Wiggins said with a grin. "Come on, Sparrow. Bring that sack over here."

Wiggins reached in above the fireplace and pulled out the bundle of rags that Queenie had stuffed into the chimney to block it. He dropped it carefully into the sack which Sparrow was holding open. Some soot fell down too, but he managed to catch most of it.

"T'riffic!" Wiggins said. "Worked like a dream. Couldn't have done it better myself. Well done, Victoria."

He ducked as Queenie swung a slap in his direction. Sparrow looked puzzled.

"Who's Victoria?" he asked.

"Never you mind," she said. "Are we finished in here?"

"We are," said Wiggins. "I've seen what I needed to see."

"So you know who done it?" Queenie asked.

He shook his head. "Not yet. But I know who didn't."

"Who's that?"

"Polly. She had coal dust all over her fingers, right?"

"Right," said Queenie. "You can see the black marks she made on the dressing table."

"Right. Now look at the black marks on the jewel box."

"There ain't none."

"Exac'ly! Whoever lifted the jewels out of it, they had clean hands. So it couldn't have been Polly, could it?"

"Cor, that's clever," said Sparrow. "Are you gonna tell the inspector?"

"Not yet." Wiggins turned to Queenie. "What's the room underneath this one?"

"The drawing room."

"What, like an artist's studio?" Sparrow asked. "Where they draw pictures?"

"No, silly," Queenie answered. "It's what the nobs call the parlour, only bigger."

"I'd like to take a look at it," said Wiggins. "There might be some clues there."

Nearly as Good as a Photo

Beaver and Gertie followed Gerald through the streets, watching his every move. Beaver noticed that as soon as they were out of sight of Mountjoy House, the easy smile vanished from Gerald's face and he looked tense and worried. After a while they found themselves in a poorer area, where the men wore cloth caps instead of top hats and the women were wrapped in woollen shawls rather than smart coats. At last, Gerald stopped outside a shop and peered in through the window. After looking cautiously over his shoulder, as though afraid someone might recognize him, he slipped quietly inside. Beaver looked up at the sign over the shop door. Hanging there were three brass balls, two at the top and one underneath.

Beaver knew what that sign meant. "It's a pawnbroker's," he told Gertie, who had caught up with him. "Where you pop things."

"What's that?" she asked.

"You give 'em things – like a watch or a coat or a ring or whatever – and they lend you money and hang on to your stuff till you pay 'em back."

"Sounds like a good idea."

"It is for the pawnbroker. You have to pay back more than they give you in the first place."

"Oh. What happens if you can't?"

"They keep your things and sell 'em."

"What d'you think Mr Gerald's doin' in there? D'you think he's poppin' Lady M's jewels?"

"I dunno. We're gonna have to find out. You stop here, on guard. I'm goin' in."

The inside of the pawnshop was like an Aladdin's cave, crammed with all sorts of things hanging from rails and heaped on shelves and piled up on the floor in glorious profusion. Hats and coats and plates and pictures, musical instruments – violins and trumpets and horns – vases and flowerpots, books and boxes, all waiting to be sold or reclaimed by their owners. At the far end of the shop was the counter. Gerald was leaning on it, speaking to an elderly man in a velvet jacket and an embroidered cap with a silken tassel hanging from it. When Beaver opened the door, a bell tinkled and the pawnbroker looked up at him through eyes as hard and shining as a hawk's.

"I'll be with you in a minute," he croaked.

Gerald did not look round. He slipped his hand in the inside pocket of his coat, drew something out and laid it on the counter.

"It's solid silver," he said. "Look, you can see the hallmarks."

Beaver crept round the side of the shop so that he could see what the object was. It was a cigarette case. The old man picked it up, examined it and sniffed scornfully.

"Not much call for something like this around here," he said, opening it and looking inside.

"That's what you always say," said Gerald.

"Thirty shillings," the man said.

"A measly thirty bob?" Gerald replied. "You can do better than that, surely? It's top quality, you know."

"Very well, two pounds, and that's my last offer. Take it or leave it."

"I'll take it."

The pawnbroker counted out coins from a drawer under the counter. While he wrote out a ticket, Beaver left the shop and rejoined Gertie outside.

"Did he have the jewels?" she asked.

Beaver shook his head. "No. I don't reckon he'd bring 'em here anyway. The jewels is worth thousands and they was arguing over a few shillings. Come on – we might as well go back."

Queenie knocked at the big double doors of the drawing room and then went in, followed by the two Boys. Lady Mountjoy was alone in the room, sitting hunched on a sofa. She had obviously been weeping – her eyes were red and she dabbed at them with a lace handkerchief that was wet with tears. But as Queenie entered, she raised her chin and sat up straight and proud.

"Yes, Queenie?" she asked.

"If you please, my lady, it's the sweep."

"Oh, yes." She smiled at Wiggins and Sparrow.

"Have you fixed the problem in my bedroom?"

"Yes, missus," Wiggins replied. "You won't have no more trouble with that."

"Very good. Thank you."

"He needs to inspect the chimney in here, my lady."

"In here?"

Wiggins stepped forward and gave a little bow. "Just to be on the safe side, lady. It uses the same flue as the one upstairs, see."

"I see. Very well."

She waved her hand towards the fireplace and Wiggins went over to it, took off his hat and knelt down to peer up the chimney.

"Well," he said. "That looks all tickety-boo, as we say in the trade. Be a shame to mess up a lovely room like this with a load of soot, wouldn't it?"

"It would indeed."

Wiggins took a good look round the room. His eyes lit up as he saw the portrait of Lady Mountjoy, and he crossed the room to stare at it.

"That's you, lady, ain't it?" he said. "Wearin' your crown, and all."

"My tiara, yes."

"Lovely picture. Nearly as good as a photograph, that is."

There was a muffled noise behind him as Queenie tried to stifle a laugh. Lady Mountjoy's lips twitched as she suppressed a smile.

"Yes," she said, "nearly as good."

Wiggins pointed a sooty finger at the picture. "I hear tell as how it's been pinched, that tiara."

"Yes, I'm afraid it has. It's very sad."

"Worth a bob or two, is it?"

"It is. But it would be very hard for the thief to dispose of. It would be instantly recognizable by any jeweller."

"Well, I'll keep my ears open, and if I hears anything... Would you be offerin' a reward for findin' it?"

"The matter is now in the hands of Scotland Yard. But if you should hear anything on your travels... Now, if you'll excuse me? Mr Harper will see to you. Queenie, take him down to the kitchen."

As Queenie closed the door behind them, they heard Lady Mountjoy laughing quietly to herself.

Queenie dug Wiggins in the ribs with her elbow.

"Wearin' her crown!" she giggled. "Nearly as good as a photo! Honest, Wiggins, I don't know what we're gonna do with you."

"Made her laugh, though, didn't I?" he grinned. "Which is better than crying. And now that I've seen a picture of the tiara, I know what we're looking for."

In the kitchen Mrs Ford was preparing a meal, but she stopped as Queenie brought Wiggins and Sparrow in.

"Well, dearie," she said, beaming at Wiggins like a fond mother. "Have you fixed it?"

"I have. All done and dusted, as they say. You won't have no more smoking up there."

"Good lad. What was the trouble?"

"Just like I said – birds. Pigeons, London starlings – they like a bit of warmth for their nests. Helps 'em to hatch their eggs quicker."

"Well, I never heard that before. Is that right?"

"Would I tell you a story?" Wiggins said, straight-faced.

"He's makin' it up!" laughed Queenie.

"You rascal!" Mrs Ford chuckled. "I suppose you'd like a cup of tea, now? Or a glass of ginger beer, perhaps?"

"Ginger beer'd be nice, thank you. Wouldn't it, Sparrow?"

Sparrow nodded enthusiastically. Mrs Ford smiled and pointed to two chairs at the table.

"Lovely. Come and sit down – only we'd better cover the chairs. Don't want soot on the seat, do we?"

"There's a paper here, Mrs Ford," said Queenie, helpfully picking up a folded newspaper from the dresser. "Shall I spread that out on them?"

"Thank you, Queenie, that'll do nicely. And I dare say this young man can manage a nice piece of veal and ham pie? Just reach one out of the pantry, will you?"

Wiggins took the newspaper from Queenie, glanced at it, then opened it out and spread two sheets on two chairs, one for himself and one for Sparrow, while Queenie went over to the pantry and came back carrying a large round pie in a dish. But as she put it down on the table, Mrs Ford let out a shriek.

"No, no!" she cried. "Not that one. I baked that special for her ladyship's birthday – it's her favourite recipe. Put it back very careful on the top shelf and fetch another."

Queenie took the pie and exchanged it for a different one, which Mrs Ford cut open and served to Wiggins and Sparrow, who tucked in ravenously.

"My goodness," Mrs Ford exclaimed. "Don't you lads get anything to eat at home?"

"Not just lately," said Wiggins. "We lost our cook." And he gave Queenie a broad wink, which set her off giggling again.

While the boys were making their way through the slices of pie, Mr Harper came into the kitchen. He was annoyed to find them sitting on his newspaper, but they smoothed out the crumpled sheets and gave it back to him only slightly dirty. Mr Harper said he supposed no harm had been done, and he paid them half a crown for clearing the blocked chimney.

"Half a crown!" crowed Sparrow when they were back outside. "We won't have to eat boiled cabbage tonight – we'll be able to buy some proper food."

"Hold your horses," Wiggins told him. "I don't think that'd be right. We ain't actually done nothing for it, have we?"

"What we gonna do, then?"

"Give it to Charlie. For lending us his barrow and his brushes. It's only fair. I mean, he ain't been able to earn nothing while we've had 'em, has he?"

Sadly, Sparrow had to agree. And anyway, he *had* just eaten a very nice slice of pie…

"He wasn't poppin' no jewels," Beaver told the other Boys when he and Gertie returned to HQ later. "Only a cigarette case, for a couple of sovereigns."

"Blimey," exclaimed Shiner. "He must be 'ard up. I wouldn't go all that way for a couple of quid if I'd got a tiara worth thousands tucked away somewhere."

"Ah, but if he's got it hid away, then he ain't got the dosh for it yet, has he?" said Rosie.

"That's right," said Sparrow, who was just leaving for the theatre. "He'd have to keep quiet and bide his time."

"'Cos if he started chuckin' his cash around, when he didn't have none before," Beaver agreed, "then everybody'd want to know where he'd got it from, and if he couldn't tell 'em, then they'd suspect him, but if he carried on as if he still hadn't got no money, then nobody would suspect him and then—"

"Right," Wiggins interrupted him. "We get the picture. Good thinking, Beav. But we don't know for sure that he done it, do we? What do you think, Polly?"

Polly had been quietly listening to the Boys as she stood at the stove, stirring a big pot of vegetables. Left on her own all day and unable to go outside in case anybody saw her, she had kept herself busy dusting and cleaning and tidying until the others could hardly recognize HQ. Now she was cooking supper. It was mainly sprouts and swedes and a few potatoes, and it didn't smell much better than last night's cabbage. But at least it was food, and it was hot, and she was doing her best with it.

"What do I think about what?" she asked.

"Mr Gerald. D'you reckon he could've done it?"

"Well, he was in the house, and his room's next to her ladyship's... He came runnin' out when she screamed and he was there when she fainted."

"Fainted?"

"Oh, yes. She was so upset she fainted clean away. Fell down on the floor, she did. Ooh, it was ever so dramatic, just like something on the stage."

"Was it, now?" Wiggins sat up straight, his eyes shining. "And her a famous actress," he said thoughtfully.

"You think she was puttin' it on?" asked Rosie. "Like, she was actin'?"

"Cor," said Shiner. "You mean she pinched 'er own jewels?"

"No, no! You can't suspect her ladyship!" cried Polly. "She wouldn't."

"Well," said Wiggins, "somebody did. There was only six people in that house, so it has to be one of 'em. We know it wasn't you, so that leaves five. Mrs Ford was downstairs in the kitchen, baking. So it wasn't her. That means it has to be one of the others: Mr Harper, Violet, Mr Gerald or her ladyship. One of 'em took the sparklers, and I reckon whoever it was has still got 'em, and they're hid somewhere in that house."

A TELEGRAM FOR MR GERALD

Next morning, the Boys took up their posts once more in the street outside Mountjoy House. Wiggins said they should take it in turns to watch the house, in case anyone got suspicious of them hanging about all day. He, Sparrow and Gertie took the first turn, so that Rosie and Shiner could carry on with their jobs in a busier street and earn a few more pennies and Beaver could get food for Polly to try to cook for supper. They had not been waiting long when the front door opened and Lady Mountjoy came out and began walking briskly along the street. Wiggins signalled to the others that he would follow her and they were to stay where they were.

Wiggins and Lady Mountjoy were hardly out of sight when someone else came out of the house, this time not through the front door but up the steps from the basement.

"It's Violet," Sparrow whispered to Gertie. "And look – she's carryin' somethin'."

It was Violet, and tucked under her arm was a package wrapped in brown paper.

"D'you think the sparklers could be in there?" Gertie asked. "In the parcel?"

"Could be. Only one way to find out – you'll have to follow her," Sparrow said. "If she sees me, she might remember me from yesterday. I'll stop here and keep an eye on the place in case anybody else comes out."

Looking quickly along the street as though making sure Lady Mountjoy had gone, Violet hurried off in the opposite direction. Gertie waited a moment, then set off after her, a few yards behind, leaving Sparrow on his own.

"Blimey," he thought. "What do I do if somebody else comes out?"

And at that very moment, somebody else did. This time it was Mr Harper, carrying not a bag or a parcel, but a letter. While Sparrow was trying to decide whether or not to leave his post and follow him, the butler stopped at the pillar box on the corner, checked the address on the envelope in his hand, touched it briefly to his lips as if he was kissing it, and popped it into the slot. Then, to Sparrow's relief, he turned and retraced his steps back to the house, looking very pleased with himself.

Wiggins was glad that Lady Mountjoy had not taken a cab, which meant, he thought, that she could not be going very far. She led him across busy Baker Street and then turned into a quieter area and rang the bell on a white-painted building with a polished brass plate beside the door. After she had gone inside, Wiggins strolled up to the door and looked at the plate. Engraved on it were the words PARKER AND MUNRO, INSURANCE AGENTS.

"Insurance," he murmured. "I dare say she'll be talking about collecting the insurance money on the jewels. Does that mean she don't expect to get 'em back?" Could Lady Mountjoy herself have faked the robbery, he wondered, so that she could get the money and still keep the jewels?

He found the idea hard to believe, but he had to admit that it was not impossible.

Gertie almost lost Violet as she made her way through a crowded street market, still clutching the brown-paper parcel. The lady's maid seemed to know a lot of the people there, who called out to her cheerfully as she passed. At the far end of the market she went into a shop selling second-hand ladies' clothes. Gertie ambled up to it and peeped in through the window. Inside she saw the shopkeeper, an enormously fat woman with crinkly black hair, greeting Violet like an old friend as she handed her the brown-paper parcel.

The woman looked around the shop to make sure no one else was inside, then waddled across, locked the door and pulled down the blind. Gertie, who had ducked out of sight, turned back and found that she could just see the shop counter through the narrow gap between blind and door. She held her breath as the shopkeeper unwrapped the parcel to reveal what was inside. Would it be the tiara?

The brown paper still hid the contents of the parcel, but whatever it was, the woman looked very pleased. However, when she lifted it out, it turned out to be a smart lady's dress, trimmed with lace. She unfolded it and held it up against Violet, examining it carefully. Then, satisfied that it was not marked or damaged in any way, she nodded and said something to Violet, who shook her head and said something in return. Gertie could not hear what they were saying, but she had been to enough horse sales with her father to know that they were haggling over money for the dress. After a few more exchanges, they obviously agreed a price and shook hands. The woman pressed a key on the ornate brass cash register, and when it opened with a sharp *ting* she took out a handful of coins and gave them to Violet, who slipped them quickly into her handbag.

When she came out of the dress shop, Violet went straight back to Mountjoy House. She did not stop, apart from calling at a little sweet shop to buy a paper bag of chocolate drops – which made Gertie's mouth water as she watched. When Violet got back, she hurried down the steps into the kitchen, where Queenie was on her hands and knees scrubbing the floor.

"Oh, look – you've made dirty footmarks all across my nice clean floor!" Queenie cried as Violet walked past her.

"So I have," Violet replied, not looking at all sorry. "You'll just have to do it again, won't you?"

Just then, Mrs Ford came into the kitchen. "What's going on here?" she demanded.

"She's walked all over my clean floor," Queenie told her.

"That's not very nice, young lady!" Mrs Ford chided Violet, wagging a finger at her. "And where have you been, may I ask?"

"Running an errand for her ladyship," Violet replied. "Is she back yet?"

"No, she ain't," Mrs Ford said, clearly not believing her. "So you ain't been missed."

"That's all right, then," said Violet with a cheeky smirk. "I'll go and take my hat and coat off before she comes back." And she trotted off into the house.

"She's getting too big for her boots, that one," said Mrs Ford, shaking her head in annoyance.

Queenie sighed and began to wipe up Violet's footprints. She looked down at her hands, which were red and sore from all the scrubbing and cleaning and washing-up she had been doing. Being a skivvy was no fun at all, she decided. She couldn't wait to get back to the Boys and HQ.

Gertie had returned to HQ to tell Wiggins and Beaver what she had seen.

"I thought it was gonna be the jewels," she said, "but it was only a frock. Mind, it looked like a very nice frock."

"Worth a bob or two?" Beaver asked.

"Yeah, I reckon it was. Real posh, if you ask me."

Polly frowned. "Violet don't have no real posh frocks," she said. "What was it like?"

Gertie was not much good at describing dresses, since she never wore one herself and wasn't very interested in them. But she did her best.

"It was made of shiny stuff. Sort of a bluey-greeny colour…"

"You mean like turquoise?" Polly asked.

"No, I don't reckon it was Turkish."

"If it was Turkish," said Beaver, "it would have had baggy trousers and a tunic – oh, and a veil. I seen a picture once of a Turkish princess, and—"

"Beaver!" Wiggins interrupted. "It ain't Turkish, it's tur*quoise*. Turquoise is a colour: bluey-green, or greeny-blue, if you like."

"Yeah, that's it," said Gertie. "And it had lots of lace down the front."

"That's one of her ladyship's dresses," exclaimed Polly. "What's Violet doin' with it?"

"Selling it, by the sound of things," said Wiggins.

"Oh, the wicked creature." Polly put her hands to her mouth in shock. "She must have stole it!"

"If Violet's a thief," Beaver said, "that means she could've stole the jewels, don't it?"

The daylight was fading into evening and the patches of mist were thickening into fog, when Shiner and Rosie saw a telegraph boy ride up the street on one of the Post Office's new red bicycles. They stared at it with great interest, fascinated at how quickly and easily it moved. The telegraph boy got off the bicycle and leant it against the railings of Mountjoy House. Shiner crossed the street to admire it. Straightening the little peaked helmet on his head, the boy climbed the steps to the front door, pulled a red envelope from the leather pouch on his belt and rang the bell. Although Shiner had never received one himself, or even seen one close up, he knew that a red envelope meant a telegram – a message sent through the Post Office that was usually urgent. Mr Harper opened the door, took the envelope and went back into the house, telling the boy to wait. Shiner scooted to the bottom of the steps.

"Psst!" he hissed. "Who's the telegram for?"

The boy shook his head. "I'm not allowed to tell you that," he said.

"Don't matter," said Shiner airily. "I know, anyway."

"Bet you don't."

"Bet I do. It's for Lady Mountjoy, ain't it?"

"That's where you're wrong," the boy replied, falling into Shiner's trap. "It's for Mr Gerald Huggett, so there!"

"Ta very much," Shiner grinned.

The boy glowered at him, but before he could retort, Mr Harper opened the door again to tell him there would be no reply. Shiner gave a cheerful wave as the boy mounted his bike again and pedalled furiously away.

"Now, who'd be sending Mr Gerald telegrams?" Wiggins mused when Shiner reported back to HQ. He turned to Polly, who was busily chopping up vegetables for supper, and asked, "Does he get many?"

Polly shook her head. "No, not that I can remember. Letters, yes. But you only send telegrams when it's something important."

"That's what I thought," said Wiggins. "Wish I could find out what it said. Might be just what we need to know."

As it happened, Wiggins's wish was about to come true. Queenie had heard the telegraph boy arrive and knew that Mr Harper had taken the telegram upstairs to Gerald's room. When she heard Gerald come down to the drawing room, she picked up her bucket of coal and climbed the stairs as quickly as she could and knocked on the door of his room, just in case. She waited a few moments and, when there was no answer, went in.

Putting the bucket down by the fireplace, Queenie quickly looked around, hoping Gerald might have left the telegram on his dressing table or writing desk, so she could read it. To her disappointment she could not see it anywhere. She even dared to slide open the drawers – taking great care not to leave dirty fingermarks – and peep inside. But there was no sign of it. She sighed and went back to make up the fire before she left. Kneeling down by the fireplace, she spotted a screwed-up piece of paper which had been thrown onto the coals but must have fallen off before it had caught light. She opened it, smoothed out the crumpled paper and read the heading: GPO TELEGRAM. The message written underneath was short: "Tomorrow ten o'clock BHY. Be there." Queenie caught her breath. She didn't know what the message meant, but the signature at the end was familiar. It was a single letter: "M".

ENTER MORIARTY

"M!" exclaimed Wiggins. "Moriarty! I might have knowed."

"Blimey," Beaver said. "What's Moriarty got to do with it?"

"Everything, I 'spect," Wiggins replied. "No wonder it's such a mystery if he's involved."

He sucked his teeth thoughtfully, then read the telegram again, trying to make sense of it. Queenie had done well. Quickly folding it up and tucking it in her apron pocket, she had hurried downstairs to the kitchen and outside, pretending she needed to fill her bucket again from the coal cellar. She had passed the piece of paper up through the railings to Shiner, and whispered to him to run back to HQ and tell Wiggins she had rescued it from the fire in

Gerald's room. Wiggins had been pleased to receive another clue, but he was puzzled by it.

"Tomorrow ten o'clock BHY. Be there." Wiggins read the message aloud and scratched his head. "BHY," he said. "Wonder what that is? Does it mean anything to you, Polly?"

Polly shook her head. "No. Never heard of no BHY. And who's this Moriarty feller anyway?"

"Professor Moriarty's the king of criminals. He's Mr Holmes's most dangerous enemy."

"Have you come up against him before, then?"

"You could say we've crossed swords with him once or twice." Wiggins looked around at the other Boys. They all nodded solemnly.

"P'raps this time we'll manage to nail him good and proper," said Beaver.

"We gotta find 'im first," Shiner pointed out.

"D'you think this BHY's a place?" asked Rosie. "*Be there*, it says. Be where? At BHY, wherever that is, right?"

"Right," Wiggins agreed. "Good thinking, Rosie. If we could work out what the letters stood for …"

"... we could suss it out and be there afore him!" cried Beaver enthusiastically. "And if he's takin' the jewels, we could see who he's givin' them to and jump in and grab 'em and..."

"Whoa, whoa!" Wiggins cut him off. "Hang on, Beav! We ain't sussed out nothing yet."

"Oh. No. Nor we ain't."

"Never mind, Beav," Gertie said cheerfully. "That's what we can do when we *have* worked it out."

"BHY," Wiggins muttered. "BHY... It's like trying to play 'I spy with my little eye'."

"Yeah – with a blindfold on," said Shiner gloomily.

"I'm gonna have to think about this," Wiggins went on. "You lot better go to bed and let me get on with it."

He went to pick up his deerstalker hat and pipe from the shelf where they lived. To his horror, they were not there. This was terrible – how would he be able to think properly without them?

"Where've they gone?" he gulped. "Mr Holmes's hat and pipe? I gotta have 'em!"

The other Boys were aghast, knowing how important they were when Wiggins had a problem to solve.

"Oh, those old things," said Polly. "I cleared them away when I was tidying up."

"You didn't … you didn't chuck 'em out, did you?" Wiggins asked fearfully.

"No, course not. I put 'em in that box of clothes over there."

Wiggins sighed with relief, dashed across the room to the box and rummaged inside it until he found the missing items. Pulling the hat firmly on his head, he gave Polly a stern look.

"Don't ever do that again!" he told her. "Why are you always trying to tidy everything up? You ain't our mother."

Polly's lips trembled and she looked as though she might burst into tears.

"I- I'm sorry," she stammered. "I don't have anythin' else to do while you're out all day. And I was only tryin' to make the place nice for you."

"Course you was," Beaver said soothingly. "You didn't have to shout at her, Wiggins. She's only doin' her best."

The other Boys all agreed, and Wiggins backed away sheepishly.

"Sorry," he grunted. "I didn't mean to, er… Sorry. Go on, now, all of you. Get to bed."

Wiggins flung himself into his special chair and prepared for another night of thinking. But hard as he tried, he couldn't find an answer to the problem. When morning came he told the others that the only thing they could do was watch out for Gerald leaving Mountjoy House and follow him when he did.

"We'll just have to let him lead us to wherever he's going," he said.

The fog had thickened during the night. As the Boys took up their positions in the street outside Mountjoy House, it lay over London like a woolly blanket. But unlike a blanket, it did not keep them warm, and they shivered in the morning chill.

"We'll warm up when we start movin'," said Sparrow, trying to stay cheerful.

"Can't be no colder than hangin' about 'ere," grumbled Shiner. "I hope 'e comes out soon."

"And he'd better not go too fast when he does," said Wiggins. "Don't want to lose him in this blooming fog."

"Yeah," Beaver agreed. "Can't see to the end of the street. We'll have to stick close to him."

"Right, but not too close. He mustn't know we're following."

"And not all in one bunch," added Gertie. "We'd better split up into two lots, three of us in each."

"Yeah. He'd be sure to notice six of us all together if he looked round," Rosie said.

"All right, let's split up now," Wiggins told them. "Beaver, Rosie, Shiner, you go on the other side of the street. Sparrow and Gertie stay with me."

They had only just separated when the front door of Mountjoy House opened and Gerald came out. He pulled on a pair of gloves, wrapped his scarf more firmly around his neck and set off at a brisk pace. The two groups of Boys followed, trying to look casual.

Keeping Gerald in sight was quite easy at first, since there weren't many people on the quiet streets. When he reached Baker Street, with its crowded pavements, it became much harder, but the Boys still managed. Then he stepped out into the road, hailed a hansom cab and climbed into it. Wiggins was quite close behind him, but not close enough to hear the address he gave to the driver. All the Boys could do was trot along behind the cab and hope they could keep up with it.

Fortunately the traffic was heavy, as usual. The streets were packed with cabs and carriages, vans and omnibuses, and the fog made them all go slower than normal, so the Boys were able to keep the cab in view. Their only fear was that with so many cabs all looking the same, it would be easy to mix them up and follow the wrong one. From behind, they could not see Gerald inside it. But luckily the cabbie, perched high up on his seat at the back, had a big red scarf wrapped round and round his neck and mouth and they kept their eyes fixed on that.

Wherever Gerald was going, it seemed a long way. The cab headed east towards the City, past the shops and new department stores of Oxford

Street and on for nearly two miles. They were not far from Newgate Prison and St Paul's Cathedral when the cab – and all the other vehicles around it – came to a complete standstill in a massive traffic jam.

Wiggins pulled out his battered pocket watch and consulted it.

"Wherever he's going," he told Sparrow and Gertie, "he ain't gonna be there by ten o'clock, unless he gets a move on."

"Looks like he knows that," Sparrow answered.

Ahead of them, Gerald had leapt out of the cab, handed some money up to the driver and set off on foot, almost running in his hurry. Signalling to Beaver and the others to cross over, Wiggins followed. They came to a shiny new red-brick office building, tall, ornate and glowing; the sign over the main entrance proclaimed it to be the headquarters of a big insurance company. For a moment, Wiggins wondered if this might be where Gerald was going – perhaps he, like Lady Mountjoy, was hoping to claim insurance money for the jewels. But instead of entering,

Gerald walked straight past and turned into a small street alongside it. The Boys followed, as closely as they dared, and soon found themselves plunged into a maze of alleyways, with ancient buildings leaning out crazily over their heads.

Gerald obviously knew the area well, and he scuttled round its many twists and turns so quickly that it became more and more difficult to track him. The fog was thicker still in the narrow lanes, and soon it swallowed him completely. Trying to guess which way he had gone in the gloom, the Boys took a wrong turning and found themselves facing a blank wall.

"Oh, no!" wailed Rosie. "We lost him."

"Don't panic," said Beaver. "He's gotta be round here somewhere."

"He must've gone the other way at that last corner," said Wiggins, heading back. "Come on. Quick."

After two turnings they came out of the alleyways into a wider street, where the fog was not so dense. Even so, they could see no sign of Gerald.

"He can't have gone far," Wiggins said. "We

only lost him for a few seconds."

"Where are we?" asked Gertie.

"It says 'Hatton Garden' up there," said Sparrow, pointing to a street sign on a nearby building.

"Don't look much like no garden to me," said Shiner. "It's all houses and shops."

"Yeah, but look at the shops," Rosie said. "They're all jewellers."

The Boys looked around them. Sure enough, nearly all the shops on the street were selling rings and necklaces and watches.

"And look at them geezers!" Beaver exclaimed.

Among the people standing or strolling around were several men dressed in black. Some were wearing fur bonnets, but most of them wore wide-brimmed black hats from which their hair hung down in curled dark ringlets. Under their full-skirted coats they wore white shawls with long fringes. They had tight stockings to their knees instead of long trousers. To the Boys, who had never seen anything like it before, they looked strange and rather sinister.

"Wiggins," Rosie whispered, "have you noticed that one over there? I reckon he's watchin' us."

The man she was talking about was standing in a shady doorway, a little apart from the others. Wiggins glanced quickly in his direction, trying not to let the man see him looking.

"Yeah, you could be right. Rum looking cove, ain't he? Wonder what his game is. Wonder what they're all doing, come to that."

His question was answered a moment later when two of the men approached each other. They greeted one another warmly and began talking earnestly in a foreign language. As the Boys watched, one of them drew a fold of paper from his inside pocket and opened it on his hand to show its contents. The other man nodded, reached out and picked up something small from it. He held it up to the light, then inspected it through a small magnifying glass which he screwed into his eye.

"It's a diamond!" gasped Rosie. "They're sellin' diamonds!"

"Now we know what Gerald's doing here," said Wiggins. "We must be in the right place."

"If only we could find him," said Beaver.

"Fat chance," Shiner groaned. "'E could be anywhere."

"That's enough of that," Wiggins said sharply. "Keep looking. He could be in any of these shops – spread out and look in all the windows!"

On Wiggins's order, the six Boys separated and began working their way along the street as fast as they could. But they couldn't see Gerald in any of the shops. They met up again on a corner, all shaking their heads.

"D'you think there's any more streets like this one?" Gertie asked.

Wiggins shrugged and scratched his head, looking around for some indication. Suddenly he stiffened with excitement and pointed at the street sign on the corner.

"Look!"

The others looked.

"*Greville Street,*" Beaver read. "What about it?"

"Go on. Read the next bit."

"Er, *Leading to Bleeding Heart Yard*?"

"Coo, that sounds spooky." Rosie shuddered.

"Never mind spooky – think about the words. Bleeding Heart Yard."

"Gotcha!" Sparrow yelled. "BHY!"

"Exac'ly! The telegram – BHY. Be there. Come on!"

Wiggins led them along the little street and into a cobbled courtyard lined with stables and workshops. On the opposite side of the court-yard a black carriage was parked, its coachman dozing on the box. As they crept towards it they could make out the monogram painted on the door – it was the familiar curly "M". Beyond the coach, behind a line of railings, they could see into the lit window of a workshop. On the work-bench, resting on a raised stand, was a piece of jewellery. Wiggins recognized it straight away from the portrait of Lady Mountjoy.

"That's it," he whispered. "That's the Mount-joy tiara!"

BLEEDING HEART YARD

"We gotta get that tiara outta there," Wiggins whispered.

"Right," said Beaver. "But how? That window's got bars on it, look."

"We couldn't reach it anyhow, with them railings there," said Shiner.

"And the front door looks like it's locked," said Rosie.

"That coachman would see us tryin' to get in, anyway," Shiner added.

"Hang on," Wiggins said. "I'll think of something."

"You'd better hurry up," said Sparrow. "Look!"

Through the barred window they saw three men enter the room and stand around the workbench, looking at the tiara. One, with his back to them, was a tall, gaunt man with a bald head. "Moriarty," muttered Wiggins. Facing him was a small man with a face like a weasel and a pointed goatee beard, blinking through steel-rimmed glasses that had lenses as thick as bottle bottoms. He was wearing a brown apron and a shiny green eye-shade. The third man was Gerald Huggett.

Although the Boys could not hear what was being said, the men were clearly in the middle of an argument. Gerald seemed to be pleading with Moriarty, who leant forward and poked him threateningly in the chest with a bony finger. Gerald shrank back, nervous and afraid, shaking his head and holding up his hands helplessly.

"Something's wrong," said Wiggins. "Looks like Gerald's in trouble."

"Shall I get the coppers?" asked Rosie.

"No. By the time you've found one, they could be long gone. And the tiara with 'em."

"What we gonna do, then?" Beaver wanted to know.

Wiggins thought as hard as he could. Then he grinned.

"Got it! Listen careful now, and I'll tell you…"

Gertie crept forward with all the stealth she had learned from her father when he'd been avoiding gamekeepers on country estates. The others held their breath as she reached out and stroked the horse and whispered in its ear to keep it calm. Then, while the coachman still dozed in his seat, she silently unbuckled the harness attaching the horse to the carriage, and gave the others the thumbs-up.

Wiggins had strolled over to the other side of the workshop door, and he now leant carelessly against the wall. When he saw Gertie's thumbs-up, he raised his hand to the others and hissed, "Go! Now!"

At Wiggins's signal, they all sprang onto action. Rosie started screaming at the top of her voice. Sparrow and Shiner began a mock fight over her, shouting and yelling as loudly as they knew how. Gertie gave the horse a smack on its rump and yelled, "Giddy up!" It lunged forward, careered off across the yard and out through the entrance. The bewildered coachman woke with a start as the shafts of the carriage crashed to the ground.

He stumbled down from his seat and began to chase after the horse. Beaver hurled a large brick at the workshop window and it shattered, spilling broken glass everywhere.

The three men inside turned angrily, then rushed out of the door and into the yard to see what was going on. As they came out, Wiggins nipped behind them, through the open door and into the workshop. He grabbed the tiara from its stand, turned it on its side and slipped it through the bars on the broken window, then tossed it to Beaver who was waiting on the other side.

As soon as Beaver had disappeared into the fog, Wiggins let out a piercing whistle and yelled, "Scatter!" The rest of the Boys stopped their fighting and screaming and ran for the narrow exit from the yard. Wiggins rushed to the door, but his whistle and shout had alerted the three men, who turned and saw the empty jewellery stand through the window. As Wiggins came out, they saw him and lined up to stop him. There seemed to be no escape. But just as one of them was about to grab this scruffy boy who seemed to have appeared from nowhere, he was interrupted by a cry from behind.

"Oy, oy, oy! Vot's going on here?" The newcomer was an old man, bowed down with age, wearing a big black hat and long coat and shaking his heavy stick at them. It was the diamond dealer who had been watching the Boys in the street. "Vot is all this shemozzle?" he demanded in a high voice.

"He's a thief!" cried the jeweller.

"Ha! And what has he stolen?"

"A tiara," said Gerald. "A diamond tiara."

"Ah. This I would like to see. Show me, please, young man."

"Don't know what you're talking about," said Wiggins. He held out his hands, then opened his coat and turned out his pockets. "See? Nothing."

"He must have passed it to one of his gang," growled Moriarty.

"Vot gang?" the old man asked. "I see no gang."

"They've run off," cried Gerald. "You must have seen them. Which way did they go?"

"Ach, die kinder." The old man nodded. "The

children. Ja, I see dem. Dey run every vich vay, into de fog. You never catch dem now."

"What are we going to do?" Gerald whined.

"Hold your tongue and keep quiet," Moriarty snapped.

"Need police," the old man said. "I call police now, yes?"

"No. No police," snarled Moriarty. "I will deal with this myself."

"But, sir…"

"I said no police. Now be off with you. Go on – clear off!"

The old man shrugged. "Very vell. Come, young man, you come vis me."

He took hold of Wiggins's wrist before the other three could do anything about it, and began leading him away. Wiggins was surprised to find that the frail old man had a grip like steel. He was even more surprised when the man spoke to him in a familiar voice, too quietly for the other men to hear.

"Keep walking, Wiggins. And don't look back."

"Mr H…!"

"Ssh. Say nothing."

As they left, the coachman was returning with his horse. He would have blocked their way, but Moriarty waved him away, and Wiggins and Mr Holmes walked steadily out of the yard and back into Hatton Garden.

The other Boys had run from the yard and ducked into the maze of alleyways across the street. Following Wiggins's orders, they scattered, all in different directions. Anyone trying to catch them would not have known which one had the tiara, or which one to follow, even if they could see them. The fog that had been their enemy was now their friend. Melting into the murky gloom, Beaver knew that no one would be able to track him as he ran. But to be on the safe side he hid the tiara under his coat and kept a tight grip on it all the way home.

Because he had gone straight to HQ, while the others had taken round-about routes to throw off any pursuers, Beaver was first back. After running almost non-stop from Bleeding Heart Yard, his legs felt bendy as rubber when he crashed through the door. He fell into Wiggins's special chair, puffing so hard he couldn't speak. He was so out of breath that Polly thought he must be ill – or at least in mortal danger.

"Beaver!" she cried. "What is it? Here, let me get you a drink of water."

"I'm all right," he panted, shaking his head. "Everything's all right. Look!"

He reached inside his coat and pulled out the tiara. Polly let out a scream.

"That's it!" she yelled. "That's the Mountjoy tiara! Oh, Beaver – you got it! You're wonderful!"

She threw her arms around him and hugged him in relief. Then she burst into tears. She was still sobbing and laughing at the same time when the rest of the Boys returned. Beaver put the tiara on her head and they all danced round the room together.

Suddenly the door opened again. They stopped dancing and stared in shock at the strange man who stood there, regarding them with an amused smile behind his straggly beard. Beaver grabbed the tiara from Polly's head and held on to it tightly.

"It's him!" shouted Sparrow. "The geezer what was eyeballin' us in Hatton Garden!"

The man gave a surprisingly hearty laugh.

"Indeed it is!" he said. "Well done, Sparrow. Excellent observation." And he stepped inside, smiling broadly. Wiggins followed him into the room, his grin stretching from ear to ear.

"Mr Holmes!" Beaver exclaimed.

While the Boys crowded round the great detective, Polly stood alone, quite confused.

"Mr...?" she stammered. "Who?"

"This is Mr Sherlock Holmes, Polly," Wiggins explained.

"Master of disguise," added Sparrow admiringly. "Cor, Mr Holmes, that's gotta be the best yet."

"Why, thank you, Sparrow," Mr Holmes replied. "And you must be Polly," he said, turning to her. "Wiggins told me all about you on our way back here."

He took off his big black hat and the side curls came off with it. Then he peeled off the false beard and rubbed his bare chin.

"Ah." He sighed with relief. "That's better.

These theatrical beards can be very itchy. Now then, let me see this famous tiara."

He held out his hand and Beaver passed it to him. Mr Holmes looked at it and smiled.

"Well done, everybody. I congratulate you all on an excellent piece of detection … wait a moment, though."

His smile turned to a frown as he looked at the tiara more closely. Then he reached into his waistcoat pocket and took out a small black tube with a lens in it, like the one the diamond merchants had used in Hatton Garden.

"What's that?" Shiner wanted to know.

"It is what is known as a jeweller's loupe. A small, high-powered magnifying glass."

He held it up to one eye and examined the tiara through it.

"As I thought," he said. "Paste."

"Paste?" asked Wiggins. "What's that mean?"

"It means, I fear, that these are not diamonds but pieces of polished glass. This tiara is a worthless fake."

A NICE PIECE OF PIE

"If this tiara ain't worth nothing," Wiggins said, "then what's all the fuss been about?"

"What, indeed?" said Mr Holmes.

"You mean we've all been chasin' about lookin' for bits of glass?" Shiner grumbled.

"Only if it was a fake all along," said Beaver thoughtfully.

"Good thinking, Beaver," said Mr Holmes. "Please continue."

"Well, p'raps the tiara what Polly saw was the real thing. And that's what was pinched."

"Right," said Wiggins. "What d'you reckon, Polly? What was it like?"

Polly thought for a moment, and her eyes became dreamy with the memory. "It was the most beautiful thing I ever saw," she said.

"But what about the sparklers?"

"Yes, tell us about the sparklers – er, the diamonds," Mr Holmes said.

"They was brilliant. When the light caught 'em, they flashed like … like … like bits of lightning in the sky."

"Well said. An excellent description of first-rate stones. Now look at these."

He held the fake tiara up to the candlelight.

"No." Polly shook her head. "I can't see no fire in them."

"Exactly. I believe we may safely assume that this is not the tiara that was stolen, but a clever copy."

The Boys all frowned at this new idea, which to most of them did not make any sense.

"I don't get it," said Gertie. "Why would anybody want a copy?"

"To swap it for the real one!" cried Wiggins.

"Precisely," said Mr Holmes.

"But why?"

"Elementary, my dear Wiggins. Consider the matter carefully."

Wiggins's forehead furrowed as he thought

hard, then his face cleared. "So they could sell the real one without anybody knowing!"

"Exactly. I understand that Lady Mountjoy is short of money."

"That's right," piped up Polly. "She's so hard up, she hasn't been able to pay Mr Harper and Mrs Ford their wages for ages. I heard them talkin' about it."

"Oh, yeah," grinned Shiner. "Listenin' at the keyhole, was you?"

"No, I wasn't. I don't do things like that. But when you're livin' in the same house, and their rooms is right next to yours, you can't help overhearin' sometimes."

"Course you can't," said Beaver.

"What happened to all the money, then?" Sparrow asked. "I mean, with her bein' a lady and all, she must've had a bob or two after her old man kicked the bucket."

"I expect she spent it all helping Mr Gerald," said Polly. "He's always getting into trouble."

"I told you he was a bad egg, didn't I?" Gertie said. "I can always spot 'em."

"But if she'd got her jewels, why couldn't

she just sell 'em?" asked Rosie.

"Not allowed to," said Polly. "I dunno why, really – I heard as they'd got tails on 'em or somethin'."

Mr Holmes smiled. "Ah. You mean they are entailed."

The Boys all looked at him, puzzled.

"It's a legal term," he explained. "It means they belong to the family and must be passed on to the next generation."

"Master Maurice, you mean? He's her ladyship's stepson. He's away at school."

"Exactly. He will no doubt inherit them when he comes of age. Until then, they must be kept safe."

"So the only way Gerald or Lady M could raise a bit of ready cash on 'em," said Wiggins, "would be to sell 'em in secret and put the fakes in their place so nobody'd know!"

"Precisely, my dear Wiggins. I sense the hand of Professor Moriarty in all this. I suspect that Moriarty discovered Gerald was in serious trouble, with debts that he could not possibly pay. He may even have tricked him into those debts himself – it would not be the first time that evil genius has ensnared some foolish young man – and then offered to rescue him, at a price. And the price was…"

"The Mountjoy tiara!"

"Well done, Wiggins. Moriarty had a copy made – no doubt he has a hold on some poor unfortunate craftsman who is able to make such pieces for him. In fact, the very reason I was in Hatton Garden in disguise was to investigate the recent discovery of a number of similar forgeries. Now, thanks to you, my Boys, I have the answer."

Everybody smiled happily – except for Sparrow, who scratched his head and looked puzzled.

"Somethin' I don't understand," he said. "If Gerald went to meet Moriarty to do the swap, why didn't he take the real tiara with him?"

There was a moment's silence as the others all thought about this. Then Wiggins's face lit up.

"'Cos he didn't have it," he said. "And he didn't have it 'cos it wasn't him what stole it! Somebody else beat him to it!"

Everyone stared at Wiggins, their mouths wide open.

"Who?" they chorused.

"And what they done with it?" asked Polly.

"I believe I know where it is," Wiggins said, "and if I'm right, you'll know who took it."

"Where is it, then?" Sparrow wanted to know.

"It's still in the house. Come on, let's get round there."

"One moment, Wiggins, if you please," said Mr Holmes. "If you are about to unmask the villain, it would be as well to have the police there."

"Good thinking, Mr Holmes," said Wiggins.

Mr Holmes gave him a stern look, but the corners of his mouth twitched as he suppressed a smile. He pulled a notebook and pencil from the pocket of his coat and quickly wrote a message in it. Tearing out the page and folding it in half, he handed it to Shiner.

"Run to the police station with this," he ordered, "and give it to the officer in charge. Tell him to come to Mountjoy House at once and meet me there."

"Gertie, you go with him. In case," Wiggins added.

"In case of what?"

"Just in case, right? Go on – off you go, and look sharp about it."

Violet opened the front door of Mountjoy House and stared at the gaggle of people standing there.

"Yes?" she demanded in a curt voice. "What do you want? Tradesman's entrance is down the steps."

"I am not a tradesman," Mr Holmes informed her. "And I wish to speak to your mistress."

"What about?" Violet asked suspiciously. Then she saw Polly. She turned and shouted into the house, "My lady! My lady! Come quick! They've got her!"

Lady Mountjoy appeared at the top of the grand staircase behind Violet. Mr Holmes and the Boys stepped quickly into the hallway.

"What is it, Violet? Who are these people?" Lady Mountjoy asked. Then, as she caught sight of Polly, she let out a little cry. "Oh! They've caught her! Quick, Violet. Send for the police."

"The police are already on their way, Lady Mountjoy," Mr Holmes told her.

"Who are you, sir?"

"My name is Sherlock Holmes. Pray forgive the costume, I had no time to change."

"Mr Sherlock…? I thought for a moment … at first sight, you reminded me of Sir Henry Irving, when he played Shylock in *The Merchant of Venice*."

"Thank you, madam. I am deeply flattered." Mr Holmes bowed his head slightly at being compared to England's greatest actor. "But when I perform, my audience is not usually aware that I am acting. Nor, I believe, is yours."

Lady Mountjoy stiffened and her lips tightened. But before she could answer, Mr Harper came out of the drawing room.

"What on earth…?" he exclaimed.

"This is Mr Sherlock Holmes, the great detective. He has brought back our thief."

"No, madam," Mr Holmes corrected her. "I am bringing back an innocent girl."

"Stuff and nonsense!" Mr Harper declared.

"We all know she stole the jewels."

"You know nothing of the sort. As my young associate, Wiggins here, will prove."

Wiggins stepped forward. Lady Mountjoy peered at him curiously. Violet looked puzzled. Mr Harper's jaw dropped and he pointed an accusing finger.

"I've seen you before!" he said. "You're the chimney sweep!"

Wiggins took an exaggerated stage bow.

"Another fine performance, I have no doubt," said Mr Holmes. "Now, Wiggins, where would you like to begin?"

"In the kitchen, if you please, sir."

"Very well. Everyone down to the kitchen. Ah, Lestrade – just in time. Please join us."

Inspector Lestrade had just arrived in the open doorway, with Shiner and Gertie and two uniformed constables. He recognized the familiar voice but stared at the strange figure.

"Mr Holmes?" he asked. "Is that really you?"

"Yes, yes. I'll explain later. Come along, now."

Lestrade signalled to the constables to stay on guard at the door while he followed everyone else down the stairs to the kitchen. Mrs Ford cried out in alarm as they all trooped in. Queenie was at the sink, washing-up yet again. She beamed at the Boys in delight.

"What's going on? What are you all doing in my nice clean kitchen?" Mrs Ford grumbled. And then, catching sight of Wiggins, "And what are *you* doing here?"

"I've come for a nice piece of one of your pies, Mrs Ford," he replied. "Queenie, would you fetch one out of the larder, please? The big one at the back of the top shelf, if you don't mind."

Mrs Ford had suddenly turned pale.

"No, no. Not that one," she cried. "That one's special."

"I thought it was," said Wiggins as Queenie returned with the pie. "Just put it down there, Queenie, and we'll take a look at the special filling, shall we?"

He picked up a large knife from the table and raised it high in the air, as if he was going to stab it into the middle of the pie. Mrs Ford let out a shriek.

"No! No, be careful…"

Wiggins lowered the knife and used it to gently lever off the pastry crust on the top of the pie. "He put in his thumb," he chanted, "and pulled out … no, not a plum, a diamond tiara! Well, what do you know? It's been hiding in there all this time, along with some rubies and emeralds and stuff. Oh, and one pearl earring. The other one was planted in Polly's box, to make it look like she was the thief, weren't it, Mr Harper?"

There was a gasp from everyone in the room, then the Boys burst into applause, as if clapping a particularly clever conjuring trick. Mrs Ford dropped heavily into a chair, covering her face with her hands and sobbing as though her heart would break. Mr Harper shuffled across and put his arm around her shoulders to comfort her. He was no longer the proud and confident butler but a broken, beaten man.

"There's your thieves, Inspector," Wiggins said. "They was planning to use the money to buy a little hotel in Brighton."

Mr Harper looked up, amazed.

"How did you know that?" he asked.

"Easy," said Wiggins. "When I was in here after

I pretended to clear the chimney in her ladyship's room, Mrs Ford made me spread a newspaper on the chair to stop it getting dirty with the soot from my trousers."

"So?"

"I noticed it was the *Brighton Echo*, and you'd drawn a ring around an advert for a hotel for sale."

"Well spotted, Wiggins!" said Mr Holmes.

"That started me thinking. But I couldn't put two and two together till just now, after we got the fake tiara out of that jeweller's workshop."

"Go on. How did you get it out?"

"I chucked it through the window to Beaver – he was waiting outside to catch it. And I suddenly thought, that's it! If I could chuck it out the window there, somebody could've done the same here. And I remembered that when I looked down out of Lady M's bedroom window, it was the kitchen area what was underneath. And then I remembered something else. When I was down there, I'd noticed a white handprint on the wall, like somebody had leant on it to steady their self while they was looking up. It was flour. So whoever it was, had flour on their hands – and that could only be Mrs Ford, 'cos she's always baking. And what was she baking? A pie. A big, round, pastry pie. This one! All she had to do was stand there and hold her apron out to catch the jewels, then pop them into the pie dish and stick the top on."

The Boys burst into applause again. Inspector Lestrade shook his head in amazement. And Mr Holmes smiled and nodded proudly. "Well done, Wiggins," he said. "You are an excellent pupil. I could hardly have done better myself."

Lady Mountjoy stood still, looking very sad. She shook her head at the butler and the cook.

"How could you?" she asked.

"You hadn't paid us for months," Mr Harper replied.

"I would have done," she said. "As soon as I was able."

"We couldn't wait. We wanted to get married and have a home of our own, before it was too late."

"Well, it's too late now," said Inspector Lestrade. "You're both under arrest."

"I trusted you both," Lady Mountjoy said. "And this is how you repay my trust."

Wiggins cleared his throat.

"Erm … I got something else to tell you, Lady M. They're not the only ones."

"What do you mean?"

"Violet's been taking your frocks and selling 'em."

To his surprise, Lady Mountjoy only smiled.

"I know," she said. "She was doing it for me. To make a little extra cash in secret. Violet has always been loyal to me – even though she was hoping to run away with my brother one of these days."

Violet blushed a deep scarlet. Mr Holmes nodded.

"Where is your brother now?" he asked.

"I don't know. He went out this morning and has not yet returned."

"No." Holmes nodded gravely. "And I very much doubt he will. If he has any sense at all, he will run and keep on running for as long as he is able. Otherwise I shudder to think what will become of him – not from the law but at the hands of the villains he has crossed."

"Oh, poor Gerald," said Lady Mountjoy sadly. "What will he do? He's not wicked, you know, just foolish. I blame myself for being too soft on him, but it was hard not to be. He was my little brother, and I had to be like a mother to him after our parents died."

"You need not reproach yourself on that score, Lady Mountjoy. He will have to learn to stand on his own two feet, which will do him no harm. There is someone else in this room, however, to whom you should make amends. If it had not been for the efforts of my young irregulars, she would have been marked for ever as a thief."

Mr Holmes gestured towards Polly. Lady Mountjoy nodded.

"I'm truly sorry, my dear," she said. "I should have believed you. What can I do to put things right?"

"Well, you could give her her job back, for a start," Queenie piped up. "That's if she wants it."

"Oh, yes, please," said Polly. "I'd like that."

"But what about you, Queenie?"

"Me? I don't want it. I've got my own job to do, lookin' after my little brother and all our friends."

"You're comin' back?" asked Shiner, a huge grin spreading across his face. "Can we 'ave one of your stews tonight?"

Everyone laughed. Mr Holmes held up his hand.

"I don't know about that," he said. "It has become our custom to celebrate your triumphs with a feast. What would you all like?"

"I'll tell you what I fancy," said Wiggins. "A nice, big, juicy steak and kidney pie – with real meat in it!"

Later that night, after stuffing themselves with pie followed by plum pudding and treacle tart with lashings of ice cream, the Boys settled into their beds ready for sleep. With Polly safely back at Mountjoy House, HQ was already getting back to its normal messy state and Beaver had to clear a space on the table before he could sit down with his exercise book and start recording the story of their hunt for the Mountjoy jewels.

Queenie crept quietly over to him and looked down at the blank page.

"What are you going to call this one?" she asked. "How about 'The Mystery of Bleeding Heart Yard'?"

"No, that'd give the game away too soon," Beaver said, chewing the end of his pencil. "We want somethin' simpler."

"All right, then," Queenie went on. "How about 'The Stolen Sparklers'?"

"Yeah," he replied. "That sounds good. 'The Case of the Stolen Sparklers' it shall be."

And he bent his head over the paper and began to write.

Hatton Garden and Bleeding Heart Yard

Hatton Garden has been London's centre for diamond trading and jewellery making for several centuries. Many dealers still trade small packets of diamonds on the street. Some of them are Hasidic Jews from Europe, who dress in black coats and wide-brimmed hats like those in our story.

Although it is now a busy street lined with jeweller's shops, the area was originally a garden on the edge of the City of London, given by Queen Elizabeth I to one of her favourites, a rich merchant called Sir Christopher Hatton, in 1581.

Bleeding Heart Yard is a real place in the centre of Hatton Garden. It is a small, quiet square, with a famous restaurant in one corner. Legend has it that the name comes from the bloody murder of Elizabeth Hatton, the beautiful wife of Sir Christopher's son. The story goes that on the morning of 26 January 1621, after a grand ball in nearby Hatton House, her body was found lying on the cobbles of the square, murdered by a spurned lover. Her heart had been torn out but was still pumping blood onto the stones.

LOOK OUT FOR THE OTHER
ADVENTURES OF

THE CASE OF THE CAPTIVE CLAIRVOYANT

THE CASE OF THE LIMEHOUSE LAUNDRY